FURIOUS JONES
AND THE ASSASSIN'S SECRET

TIM KEHOE

FURIOUS JONES

AND THE ASSASSIN'S SECRET

Simon & Schuster Books for Young Readers
New York   London   Toronto   Sydney   New Delhi

SIMON & SCHUSTER BOOKS FOR YOUNG READERS
An imprint of Simon & Schuster Children's Publishing Division
1230 Avenue of the Americas, New York, New York 10020
SIMON & SCHUSTER BOOKS FOR YOUNG READERS is a trademark of Simon & Schuster, Inc.
For information about special discounts for bulk purchases, please contact Simon & Schuster Special Sales at 1-866-506-1949 or business@simonandschuster.com.
The Simon & Schuster Speakers Bureau can bring authors to your live event. For more information or to book an event, contact the Simon & Schuster Speakers Bureau at 1-866-248-3049 or visit our website at www.simonspeakers.com.
Jacket design by Chloë Foglia
Interior design by Hilary Zarycky
The text for this book is set in Electra.
Manufactured in the United States of America
0314 FFG
2 4 6 8 10 9 7 5 3 1
Library of Congress Cataloging-in-Publication Data
Kehoe, Tim.
Furious Jones and the assassin's secret / Tim Kehoe. — First edition.
pages cm
Summary: Upon witnessing his famous spy-novelist father's murder just seven months after his mother's death, twelve-year-old Furious, now an orphan, seeks clues in his father's latest novel to stop the murderer before he or she strikes again.
ISBN 978-1-4424-7337-9
ISBN 978-1-4424-7339-3 (eBook)
[1. Murder — Fiction. 2. Spies — Fiction. 3. Authors — Fiction.
4. Assassins — Fiction. 5. Orphans — Fiction. 6. Organized crime —
Fiction. 7. Adventure and adventurers — Fiction.] I. Title.
PZ7.K25177Fur 2014
[Fic] — dc23
2013009281

FIRST
EDITION

To Sherri

Acknowledgments

The creation of Furious Jones was a team effort, and I'm fortunate to have the very best team. I am thankful for the patience of everyone at Simon & Schuster and will forever be indebted to my editor, Kristin Ostby, for her guidance and help in shaping Furious. Her instinct, intelligence, and advice took this book to entirely new levels. Thank you!

I'm lucky to have the most talented and thoughtful agent on the planet in Sloan Harris at ICM. Both Sloan and the amazing Tina Wexler spent countless hours helping me shape Furious and his world.

Finally, I would like to thank my wife, Sherri, for her tireless dedication. Her patience, partnership, and willingness to put up with loud music made this book possible.

CHAPTER ONE

My hair fell over my eyes as I crossed against the
light on Fifth Avenue. I should've gotten a haircut. It would
be the first thing out of my dad's mouth. I hadn't seen my
dad since my mom's funeral, seven months ago, and I just
knew we were going to argue about my hair. I could hear
him already. He would go on and on about appearances and
respect and all that other crap. He would use that Marine-
Corps-drill-sergeant voice. He would make it clear that he
was the world-famous adventurer, fearless explorer, tough-
guy author, and I was his screw-up son. He was never even
in the Marines. Man, what was I doing here? This was a bad
idea. My dad didn't like surprises. And he wouldn't like me
showing up like this—unannounced.

I stood in front of the hotel with my back to traffic. There were lots of people gathered around the hotel entrance. And they were all dressed up. Most of the men were wearing tuxedos, and the women were all in fancy dresses. I assumed they were all here to see my dad. I looked down at my jeans and T-shirt. A remark about my clothes would be the second comment out of his mouth. This was a really bad idea.

I walked toward the front door of the hotel and noticed two giant men on either side of the door. They looked like bodyguards. Or secret service. Did my dad have his own protection now? Was he that famous? Or had my mom's murder scared him? I doubt my dad was scared. He was the toughest guy I had ever met. Nothing scared him.

I walked past the bodyguards and stepped into the hotel lobby. The lobby looked like all the other five-star hotels my mom and I had stayed at over the years. It was full of shiny marble and shiny brass fixtures and shiny mahogany tables. There was a sign indicating that my dad's event was being held in the Grand Ballroom. I followed the crowd. Maybe I could blend in. Maybe my dad wouldn't notice me if I sat way in the back. Then I could decide if I wanted to see him or not. I looked down at my T-shirt again. It had a hole in it, just beneath the picture of a motorcycle. Blending in was going to be difficult.

What was I doing here? My dad hadn't even tried to contact me for weeks. Even when he was calling, we hardly had anything to say to each other. Man, I should turn around and go.

I looked back over my shoulder. The line stretched back as far as I could see. The crowd kept moving down the hallway toward a large set of doors, and I kept moving with it. There were several hotel employees standing in front of the doors taking tickets.

Tickets? People actually paid to see some guy read from a book? I hadn't planned this very well.

The truth was, like most things, I hadn't planned it at all. Two hours ago, I was sitting at my grandpa's kitchen table, in Connecticut, when I looked down and noticed my dad's picture in the newspaper. That was the first I'd heard about my dad's new book, *Double Crossed*. That's when I got the idea to sneak into the city and see him. My grandpa would never have let me go into the city alone. Since my mom's death, he was nervous about me being alone anywhere. I swear he freaked out a little even when I went to school.

I'd moved in with my grandpa after my mom was killed seven months ago. I'd been attending New Canaan Middle ever since. It was, like, the twentieth school I'd attended in the past six years. But it was far and away the nicest. New Canaan has to be one of the safest, and richest, places in the country. I mean, nothing happens in New Canaan. And to top it off, my grandpa was the chief of police there.

My grandpa had like a dozen guns in the house and a

police squad car in the driveway. It wasn't like anything was going to happen to me. But despite all that, he actually drove me to school for the first couple of weeks after my mom was killed. The school is, like, five blocks from his house, and he drove me every day. Don't get me wrong, I appreciated his concern, but it's a little embarrassing to have your grandpa walk you into school every morning when you're in the seventh grade.

He'd gotten a little better lately, but he'd die if he knew I was here right now. So I made up a story about going to a friend's house and got on the train. It was about an hour train ride from New Canaan to New York City, and I swear I regretted my decision about ten minutes into the ride. I didn't want to upset my grandpa, but I really missed my dad. I just wanted to see him. And hear his voice. But if he saw me here alone like this, totally unplanned and out of the blue, he would probably be mad. I figured maybe I could stand in the back of the room and just listen to his talk.

The blond woman standing in front of the large doors held out her hand and said, "Ticket, please."

"I, ah, I don't have a ticket."

"I'm sorry, but you need a ticket to attend tonight's event," she replied.

"I'm Furious Jones," I said. Man, I hated my name. I mean, who names their kid Furious? And that was my actual name. I've seen the birth certificate and everything. It says

Furious Catton Jones. I've asked my parents about it over the years—I mean, when my mom was still alive and my dad was still talking to me. Apparently I came into this world a little upset. To hear my mom tell it, I was kicking and screaming from the minute I was born, and I actually punched the doctor in the nose. My dad thought it was so funny, they decided to name me Furious. And just like that—they practically ruined my life.

The ticket woman was giving me the same look that everyone gave me when I said my name.

"Yeah, I know it's a weird name," I said. "But I'm Robert Jones's son," I said.

"Look," she said as she stopped smiling, "I'm just trying to do my job here. I can't let you in without a ticket, okay? If you really were Robert Jones's son, don't you think you'd have a ticket? Or be with him right now?"

"Yeah, you would think so, wouldn't you," I agreed. It was hard to argue with that, and it was all a bad idea to begin with. I was about to walk away when I heard—

"Did I hear you say you're Furious Jones?"

I turned around to see the two giant men from the front of the hotel standing on either side of an equally large man with thick black hair.

"Excuse me?"

The man in the middle repeated the question. "Did I hear you say your name is Furious Jones? Robert Jones's son?"

The guy looked important. I guess anyone surrounded by bodyguards looked important. But he also looked familiar. I had been cursed with a near-photographic memory since the age of six, and I knew I had seen his face before. Maybe on television?

"Yes, I'm Furious."

"Of course you are," he said as he shoved his meaty hand into mine. "You have your dad's height. What are you, six feet two?"

I was actually six feet *four*. And I was sure I had to be one of the only six-feet-four-inch twelve-year-olds on the planet. In all the schools I had attended over the years, I was always the tallest kid in the class. People were always thinking I was older than I was.

"Yeah, something like that," I said.

"Well, it is a pleasure to meet you. I'm Attorney General Joseph Como. I'm sort of a friend of your father's."

The way he said "sort of a friend" sounded odd. How is someone "sort of" a friend?

"You probably recognize me, right?" he asked.

I nodded yes. And I wasn't lying. I did remember his face, but I was pretty sure I had never heard his name. And I was positive I had no idea what an attorney general did.

"Well, I'd be honored if you would accompany me to your dad's reading."

His smile was effortless and his teeth were perfect. His

hair was perfect. I figured the attorney general had to be some sort of politician. He was probably here trying to get money from my dad for a campaign or something.

My dad was the author of the wildly popular Carson Kidd book series. I didn't know much about the books. I had never actually read one. My mom didn't want the books in the house and, since she died, I guess I just haven't wanted to read anything. I knew they were spy thrillers. And I knew all five books had been huge hits and made my dad a ton of money. There were even several Carson Kidd movies. But I hadn't seen any of those, either.

I'm not 100 percent sure why my parents got divorced, but it seemed to center around my dad's books. Or, maybe, the fame that came with the books. My dad's fame was pretty out of control. He was all over the Internet and the newspapers. And whenever I did get the chance to spend time with him, people would constantly come up to him asking for stuff. They would want to take a picture with him. Or get his autograph. Or want him to listen to their book or movie ideas. Some would just flat-out ask him for money. My mom hated that stuff. She liked to keep a low profile.

"I would love to join you," I lied. "But I don't seem to have a ticket."

"Ah, yes," Attorney General Como said as he gestured to one of the bodyguards. "Joe, would you mind waiting outside the ballroom?"

"I guess that would be okay," Joe replied.

"Thank you," Como said. "It looks like I've got an extra ticket for you, Furious."

He handed three tickets to the blond woman, put his arm around my shoulder, and we entered the ballroom together, his other bodyguard following behind us.

The room was enormous. The walls stretched up three stories high and were lined with fancy gold lights. Several hundred folding chairs had been set up in the front of the room, facing a small stage, and there must have been over a hundred people standing around talking in the back of the room. And another hundred people filing in behind us.

"So, how is it that the son of the author doesn't have a ticket?" Como asked.

"I guess because the author doesn't know his son is here," I replied. "And, I guess, the son didn't realize people actually paid to see some guy read from a book."

Como laughed. "And apparently, the son didn't realize people actually dressed up for it."

"Right," I agreed as I pushed my hair out of my eyes.

I looked pathetic standing there. Not only was I, as usual, one of the tallest people in the room, but I was also the only person dressed in jeans and a T-shirt. And I was the youngest by about forty years. It looked like my dad's book only appealed to old people. And now it seemed like all the old people were staring at me. Or rather, the guy I had entered the room with.

"Attorney General Como!" an elderly couple exclaimed as they approached us with their arms out.

"It is so lovely to see you," Como said, greeting the couple.

And then another couple approached Como. And another. And soon there was a small line of people waiting to meet him.

I wanted to run and hide, but Como kept shaking hands, smiling, and introducing me to one old person after another. And the line continued to grow, and Como continued to shake hands. Everyone was offering him best wishes and good luck. They kept saying things like: *Hang in there, The right man is going to win in the end*, and *You're going to look pretty good in that oval office.*

Oval office? That's why I recognized the guy; he was running for president. And to hear these people tell it, it sounded like he was going to win.

Great, I thought as I scanned the room for my dad. I was hoping to sneak in and listen to my dad from the back of the room, where I wouldn't be noticed, and now I was standing next to the future president of the United States.

The ballroom lights flashed several times, warning everyone it was time to take their seats. Como shook a couple more hands, and his giant bodyguard started to guide us toward the stage.

It figured. We were headed toward the front row. There

would be no way for my dad to miss me now, sitting there in my T-shirt and jeans.

"You know," I said to Como, "I'm feeling bad about taking your friend's ticket."

"My friend?" Como asked. "Oh"—he chuckled a little—"Joe's not my friend."

Then Como stopped and turned toward the bodyguard.

"No offense, Gary," Como said to the bodyguard. "You and Joe do great work."

"No offense taken, sir," the giant bodyguard said in a deep, rumbling tone. So much for me trying to get out of this.

The bodyguard then motioned for us to enter the front row. "Our seats."

Man, I knew it. We were sitting front and center. We were only a few feet from the podium that had been placed onstage.

"You might have heard that I'm running against Senator White for president," Como said, leaning toward me. In a whisper he added, "The secret service detail is just part of the package."

"Oh, the secret service. Of course," I whispered.

I sat to the left of Como, and the secret service agent took the aisle seat to his right.

"That's kind of cool," I said. "I mean, having your own secret service and all."

"It is what it is," Como replied. "In my line of work, you end up with a lot of powerful friends and powerful enemies." Then he chuckled and added, "And sometimes it is hard to tell the difference.

"Can you believe this turnout?" Como asked, looking back at the crowd as the ballroom lights dimmed.

I said nothing. I was starting to feel sick. I shouldn't be here. I needed to get out of here, but it was too late. A bright spotlight was suddenly shining on the podium, and a man was walking onto the stage.

CHAPTER TWO

Good evening and welcome," said the man onstage.
"My name is Richard Olson and I'm the executive director
for the New York Public Library. As always, I'd like to thank
all of the Friends of the Library for your continued support.
But I know you're not here to listen to me talk all night, so
let's get right to it.

"We're here tonight to celebrate the forthcoming sixth
book in the Carson Kidd series by the one and only Robert Jones." The audience erupted into applause. "Kidd is the
rough-and-tumble CIA assassin that has thrilled us, capti-
vated us, and, on more than one occasion for me personally,
robbed us of precious sleep as we lay awake turning pages.

"Kidd is tough," Olson said with a laugh. "No doubt

about it. But he's also fair. He seems to have a strong sense of right and wrong. Time after time and book after book, he stands up for those who have been wronged. And, in his patented way, he believes in righting wrongs with whatever force is necessary."

The crowd laughed and applauded politely.

"Now, I've had the good fortune to know Mr. Robert Jones for several years," the speaker continued. "And, with the possible exception of the violence, I think Robert shares many of his lead character's traits. I've witnessed Robert help those around him. I've witnessed Robert right the wrongs and stand up for those who can't stand up for themselves.

"And Robert has been a constant supporter of the library and many literacy programs not just here in New York, but across this great country."

The audience gave another round of polite applause.

Olson continued, "And now, without further ado, please help me welcome Mr. Robert Jones."

The applause grew even louder and the audience stood as my dad entered the spotlight and crossed the stage to the podium, waving to the crowd. He was about fifteen feet from me now. We hadn't been this close in seven months. Not since I'd stood next to him at my mom's funeral.

He looked tired and older than I remembered him. He had deep lines under his eyes, and his hair seemed thinner and lighter. He looked like he had aged ten years in seven months. Could my mom's death have taken that big of a toll? He certainly had not been himself since her murder. He'd called me every few days after the funeral. And he had sounded different. Paranoid. He kept asking about my safety. Was Grandpa taking me to school every day? Did he have a police officer stay at the school? Had I received any strange phone calls or messages? He kept reminding me not to talk to strangers, like I was five years old. I don't know who was worse, my dad or my grandpa. My mom's murder must have taken a toll on both of them. Well, all of us, I guess.

My dad motioned for everyone to sit down. He still hadn't noticed me in the front row. The room was dark, and the spotlight was shining bright in his eyes. Maybe he couldn't see me, and I would get away with this after all.

The room quieted and we sat.

"Thank you. It's wonderful to see so many of you here tonight. And I'd like to thank Richard and the Friends of the Library for having me here tonight.

"As I look around this room," my dad said, scanning the crowd, "and see so many familiar faces, it's hard to believe we've been doing this for over—"

My dad froze as our eyes met. The smile drained from his face.

"Ah," he tried to continue. "It's, ah, hard to believe that I've been writing these books for over six years now."

He stopped again and just stared at me. I had never seen

this expression before, but he didn't look happy to see me. The crowd started to look in my direction. And then my dad locked eyes with Attorney General Como. He stared at Como. And Como stared back. Then Como gave my dad a little wave.

My dad looked away. "And in another six years, I hope to be doing this still. I think Carson has a lot of adventures left in him."

He paused again. He looked over at me again. And then he looked down at the podium.

He said nothing.

Thirty seconds passed.

A minute passed.

A murmur started to grow from the crowd.

But he just kept staring at the podium.

I had never seen him like this.

He looked broken.

Sad.

Scared.

My dad was never scared.

Was this because of me?

What should I do?

Should I get up and go? Would he follow me? Could he? He had a room full of people here to see him. Maybe I could get back to my grandpa's house before he called. I could explain it all to my grandpa and apologize. He would see that I was okay, and I'd promise never to do it again.

I was just about to stand up when he looked forward and continued talking.

"Kidd's newest adventure has its roots in Chicago," he finally spoke. "And by definition, Chicago stinks. In the language of the Potawatomi Indian tribe, the word 'Chicago' literally means 'wild and smelly onion.' In the Algonquian tribe, the word 'Chicago' means 'smells bad.'

"The one thing historians and scholars are unclear about, however, is whether those early dwellers were referring to the wild leeks that were abundant along the river, or if it was early social commentary describing corrupt Chicago politics and the infestation of the Sicilian mafia."

The crowd started to laugh, and I stood up and walked toward the aisle.

"The new book opens in a small Illinois town," my dad said. Then he let out a large sigh. "And I've got to tell you, this is far and away my darkest and most twisted book to date. I mean, there is some truly sick stuff happening in this small town. And Carson meets his match in this book. I think the readers will be surprised—"

He paused as I started walking up the main aisle. I could feel people turning to look at me now. I tried not to make eye contact with any of them.

"Ah," my dad muttered. "Carson discovers that . . ." He paused again. "Let's just say sometimes it is hard to tell your enemies from your friends."

I stopped in the darkness.

That was odd. That was almost identical to the thing Attorney General Como had said. I turned back toward my dad when—

BANG!

BANG!

BANG!

CHAPTER THREE

*T*hree quick explosions thundered through the ball-room, and I watched my dad fall to the stage floor. I let out a scream, and then, as if time had slowed, I saw Gary, Como's secret service man, stand up. The spotlight lit his body as he stood. He had a gun in his hand and started to point it across the room, looking for the shooter.

My eyes followed the path of the gun. It pointed to a skinny man in a leather jacket standing off to the side. The skinny man's slicked-back hair shimmered in the spotlight. Did he have a gun? Had he just shot my dad?

Several more explosions rang out. These were faster and higher-pitched. Blood and brain matter seemed to hang in the air where the head of the man with the slicked-back hair had been. Then, as if someone had pushed a fast-forward button, the room erupted in chaos. People were screaming. People were crying and climbing over chairs and one another.

A mass of bodies filled the aisle and swept me out the ballroom doors.

I saw Joe, the other secret service agent, fighting the crowd in an effort to get into the ballroom. His gun was drawn, and he was shoving people out of his way. I ran down a hall I didn't recognize. And then another hall. There was a door with an EXIT sign. I went through the door and found myself in an alley.

I fell to the ground and grabbed my face and started to cry. "Oh, god! Oh, god!"

I stopped and looked around. With no one in sight, I cried harder.

"Oh my god," I cried. "Oh, god. Oh, god. Oh, god."

I tried to stop but couldn't. My eyes stung. My nose was running. Not here. Not like this.

Pull yourself together, Furious!

I sat up and wiped my nose on my sleeve. I could hear sirens coming from every direction. I wondered if I should go back inside and help my dad. There had been so much blood. There was no way he was still alive. I looked toward the street, and cop cars were trying to cut through the crowd of people in the street in front of the hotel. I needed to leave.

They would call my grandpa soon, and he would panic when he couldn't find me. I couldn't do that to him. He had already been through so much. And I didn't want him to know I'd lied to him. I had to try to get home before he got the call.

I crossed Fifth and looked back toward the hotel. A half-dozen cop cars were blocking the street, and people were pouring out of the front door. I turned and headed to the corner subway station. I could take the subway to Grand Central and then catch a train back to my grandpa's house in New Canaan.

I made my way down to the subway platform. The lights in the station were bright and my eyes burned from crying. I closed my eyes for a second and pictures of my dad's body hitting the stage were vivid in my mind. I could see the blood on his dress shirt, face, and hair. I tried to replace the image, but I knew it was pointless. I had no control over the way my screwed-up mind retained images. The picture of my dad's dead body would stick forever. Every detail would sit right next to the image I saw of my mom's dead body.

A train raced into the station and came to a quick stop. I got on and headed to the back of the car. I sprawled out on a double seat and stared out the window.

It was uncanny, I realized. My mom and dad had been killed in almost the exact same way. Three shots to the body. Both of them killed at hotels.

I wasn't there when my mom was killed. She had left me

with my grandpa while she went to some small Illinois tourist town called Galena. I guess that was the first sign that something was wrong. She had never left me behind. My mom traveled for business, and I always went with her. We had been all over the world together. But she'd been acting very strange before the trip to Galena. She had even reached out to my dad, something she had never done in the six years they had been divorced. If there was anyone on the planet tougher than my dad, it was my mom. And I was positive something was wrong as she pulled out of my grandpa's driveway. She seemed nervous. Like we were saying good-bye for the last time. And it turned out we were.

Most of what I knew about my mom's murder came from what I read in the *Galena Gazette*. Which wasn't much. The *Gazette* ran a picture of my mom's bloody body on the sidewalk in front of the DeSoto House Hotel in downtown Galena. The sheriff was quoted as saying that a car pulled up and someone opened fire. That was it. The whole thing was over in a matter of seconds, and he said that my mom had just been in the wrong place at the wrong time. But I never really believed that.

The article went on to say that, until very recently, Galena hadn't had a murder since the Chicago gangster Al Capone had used the area as a hideout seventy years ago. So it's not like drive-by shootings happened all the time there. Galena was a little town of six hundred people and no recorded violence. The shooting was not random. She was killed on purpose. But why?

My mom was an accountant. We had moved around so much, neither of us had friends, much less enemies. And judging by how nervous my dad and grandpa had been since her death, they didn't seem to believe it was random either. And now my dad was dead too.

Someone was hunting my family.

I got off at Grand Central to transfer to the New Haven line. I looked at my phone. It was 8:09 p.m. and it was an hour ride to New Canaan. The next train left at 8:30. I sat down on a bench and pushed my hair back. It immediately fell over my eyes. My long hair always bothered my dad.

I closed my eyes and images of the ballroom rushed in again. I could see my dad standing behind the podium. I could see the look of fear and sadness as we locked eyes. What was he worried about? Why had my grandpa and my dad been so worried about me? Did they know someone was after us? Was I next? Did it end with the guy with the slicked-back hair?

The train to New Canaan pulled into the station. I got on and stared out the window for the better part of an hour, thinking about my mom and dad. I suddenly realized that, technically, I was an orphan. My grandpa was the only family I had left in this world. I couldn't stop crying as the train cut through the Connecticut countryside. Should I call my grandpa? What would I say? *Hey, it's me, just checking in. I wanted to make sure you hadn't realized I'm an ungrateful liar.*

My grandpa took me in after my mom died. I guess it sort of made sense to me. I hadn't lived with my dad in years. I actually had no memory of my parents together and had only seen my dad once or twice a year since the divorce. He was busy traveling and writing his books, but I had always hoped that we would spend some time together eventually. But at my mom's funeral, my dad came up to me and said he was working on his new book and he had a lot of research to do. He said his research would take him to a dangerous place. That it wasn't safe and he would need to go there alone.

But I had spent six years traveling with my mom and we had seen all kinds of dangerous places. My mom took a job as an accountant with a government contractor after she left my dad. Her job required us to travel a lot. Her company sent us from city to city and country to country. We'd usually stay in a city or country for a few weeks and then move on. My mom would enroll me in school at the closest military base. When we weren't close to a base, she would enroll me in a local school. I was always the new kid. New teachers, books, and faces. But the same questions. Same stares. Same crap. Just a different town or country. Sometimes a different language. Often a language that I didn't even speak.

I had learned to survive dangerous places. But my dad didn't listen. At my mom's funeral he said we would talk about the "arrangement" after his book was finished. That's part of the reason I was so excited to see his book event in the paper this morning. The story said he had finished his new book and it was set to come out next week. I was hoping that maybe I could spend time with him now. But now that was never going to happen.

My phone vibrated. It was my grandpa calling. I clicked accept and held the phone to my ear.

"Hello," I said.

"Furious? Are you all right?"

"Yeah, I'm fine," I lied.

"Where are you?"

"I'm at Andy McMahon's." I squeezed my open hand into a fist as I lied again. I hated lying to my grandpa. And picking Andy's house was a huge mistake. Andy lived right next door. It wouldn't be hard for my grandpa to figure out I was lying. He could practically look out the window and *see* that I was lying.

"I need you to come home," he insisted.

I looked down at the clock on the phone. The train was still fifteen to twenty minutes from New Canaan.

"Can we just finish the game we're playing?" I asked.

There was a moment of silence and then I heard my grandpa sigh and I knew he had heard about my dad. He sounded defeated. He sounded exactly like he did after my mom was killed.

"Finish it quickly and then come straight home," he said. "Okay?"

"Okay," I said and clicked cancel on my phone.

I bit down hard on my lip to fight back the tears. Why hadn't I just told my grandpa the truth? Once you start lying, it just takes on a life of its own.

I stared at the clock on my phone thinking about my grandpa. He was a good guy. Quiet, for the most part. Very different from my dad. My dad had been larger than life. He was always putting on a show. But my mom was more like my grandpa—her dad. She never wanted to draw attention to herself. She tried to stay out of the spotlight as much as possible. In fact, my parents divorced just months after my dad's first book became a huge international bestseller. Just after the fame had started. She had only been a part of that for a few months, but she always said it was the worst period of her life.

My parents got divorced when I was six years old. And, oddly enough, I have no memories of anything before six. Not a single memory. I had seen many shrinks over the years, and many of them said six years old was psychologically the absolute worst age for a child to experience divorce. Something about the way the brain is forming at that age can cause a lifetime of difficulties. I'm no shrink, but I believed it. And they all found it fascinating that while I can't remember a thing before the age of six, I'm cursed with a photographic memory of practically everything after six. After the divorce.

I could recount every single detail of all the time I'd spent with my dad *since* the divorce. Of course, there weren't really that many times to recall. Over the years, my mom and I only saw him on the rare occasion we all ended up in the same city or country at the same time. And that had happened about a dozen times in six years. And it never went well. Well, actually, it always started out great but never *ended* well.

My dad would show up and book a room at whatever hotel my mom and I were staying at that week, and he would try to be the big man. His visits usually centered around food. My dad loved good food. No matter where we were, he would always know how to find the best food. We could be in a small town in the middle of Prague, in the Czech Republic, and my dad would say, "Oh, there's the best little place just a few blocks from here. They've got a chef named Ronald and he makes an amazing grilled sea bass." And, sure enough, the three of us would enter the restaurant and a chef named Ronald would hurry over to say hello to my dad. In the middle of Prague! That's what he did. He was always the big man putting on a big show. And, secretly, I loved it.

He was truly larger than life. But my mom said he hadn't always been that way. The Robert she fell in love with had been a kind, hardworking, and idealistic journalist. She'd tell me stories about their life in Saint Paul, Minnesota. My mom grew up in New Canaan but went away to college in Minnesota. My dad had grown up in Saint Paul, and they met at the University of Minnesota. My dad was a journalism major and my mom was studying economics and Italian. After they graduated, my dad took a job as a reporter at the *Saint Paul Pioneer Press*. And he was good at it. My mom said he loved to fight for the underdogs. He even won a big award for a series of stories that exposed some crooked politicians.

My mom claimed my dad invented the Robert Jones persona to help sell books. But then it consumed him. He bought into his own creation, she said. But so did she, from time to time. By the second or third day of his visits, the two of them would be holding hands and laughing. By the end of the first week, they would look like a couple again. We would look like a family again. And then this thing from the past would creep in. They would start to fight about my dad's fame and the books. Ultimately, my dad would leave.

The train slowed as it pulled into the New Canaan station. It was the last stop on the line, and I was the last passenger. I got off and walked the four blocks to my grandpa's house.

There was a cop car idling in the driveway behind my grandpa's squad car.

CHAPTER FOUR

My grandpa had been the chief of police in New Canaan for almost thirty years, so seeing a cop car in the driveway wasn't completely out of place. It didn't mean there was necessarily something wrong. Or that my grandpa had started a manhunt looking for his missing grandson. At least that's what I told myself as I walked through the back door.

My grandpa was sitting at the kitchen table with Lieutenant Miller.

"There you are, Furious. I told you just to finish the one game. I was starting to get worried," my grandpa said as he stood up and walked toward me.

"Sorry it took so long," I said.

He put his arm around me and gave me some sort of

half hug. We weren't a real touchy-feely family, and an arm around the shoulder was practically like a bear hug for us.

"Furious, you remember Lieutenant Miller, right?"

Of course I remembered Lieutenant Miller. This mind of mine wouldn't let me forget anything. Ever. And Lieutenant Miller was one of only a handful of cops in New Canaan. Miller had worked for my grandpa for almost twenty years.

"How are you, Lieutenant?" I asked.

Lieutenant Miller gave me a sympathetic smile. "I'm okay, Furious."

"Come on and sit down." My grandpa gestured toward the small kitchen table.

"What's going on?" I said without moving.

My grandpa let out another long sigh, and his eyes watered as he looked at me. "I'm so sorry, Furious. It's your dad. He's been shot."

My grandpa went on talking, but I didn't hear anything after the word "shot." My legs were weak and my eyes stung. Something about the words coming out of my grandpa's mouth made my dad's death more real than having seen it for myself. I started to cry, and my grandpa squeezed me harder.

Lieutenant Miller stood up and walked past us toward the back door.

"I'm going to let you two be alone, Bud. I'll stop back in the morning."

I heard the back door slam shut, and I cried even harder.

"I'm so sorry, Furious. I'm so sorry. No one should have to go through what you've been through. What *we've* been—"

My grandpa's voice cracked and he stopped talking. I stood there with his arm around me for several minutes. Images of my dad's body on the stage flooded my stupid photographic mind. And then there were the images of his face. The look of sadness and fear in his eyes when he saw me. Those were his last few feelings. He died disappointed in me. I hadn't seen my dad in seven months, and disappointment would forever be his last thought of me.

"You know I'm always here for you, right?" my grandpa said, hugging me even harder this time.

I nodded.

"We've just got each other now," he added.

The back door opened suddenly, and both my grandpa and I jumped. It was Lieutenant Miller with a man in a dark-blue suit.

"Jesus, you startled me," my grandpa said, wiping the tears from his face.

"Sorry, Bud," Lieutenant Miller said. "Ah, this is Director Douglas with the CIA. He'd like to ask you a couple of questions."

"Douglas?" my grandpa asked. "What in the world are you doing here?"

Lieutenant Miller looked confused. "You two know each other?"

"Oh yes, Lieutenant. Bud and I go way back," Douglas said as he took a step into the kitchen. He looked at me and said, "I'm sorry for your loss, Furious."

"Don't talk to him," my grandpa said as he put his arm between me and Douglas. "Don't you dare talk to my grandson."

Director Douglas wasn't a huge guy, but he looked solid. Tough. Still, I could tell he was afraid of my grandpa. And for good reason. I had never heard my grandpa raise his voice like he was now. There was pure hatred in it.

"You are not welcome here, Douglas. Now you just turn around and get out of here before I have you arrested!"

Douglas took a step backward.

"I get it, Bud. I understand how you feel, but you have to trust me on this. I need—"

"Trust you!" my grandpa roared. "That's a good one, Douglas. You're lucky I don't kill you right here." My grandpa now pushed me to the side and stood directly between Douglas and myself.

"Now, Bud, I don't think that's a—" Lieutenant Miller started to say something, but my grandpa looked at him and he stopped midsentence.

"You probably had your hands in this, too, didn't you, Douglas. I'm going to look into Robert's murder, and so help me, if—"

Douglas seemed to have lost any fear or respect that was

holding him back. He took two quick steps toward us.

"Listen," he said as he raised one finger in the air. "I understand you're grieving, Bud, and I am truly sorry for your loss. You know Terri's death was a huge loss for us, too. But I've got people who are still in real danger, and I need to get some answers."

My grandpa took a step toward Douglas. They were standing nose to nose.

"Your loss?" my grandpa questioned. "It's your fault my daughter is dead."

"What?" I asked. "What are you talking about?"

Douglas looked at me and then back at my grandpa. "Your grandpa is just upset, Furious. He's not making sense."

Douglas took another look at me and stepped back toward the door.

"I'll be back in the morning, Bud. I need to know what Furious saw. I've got people in jeopardy out there."

CHAPTER FIVE

*T**he door slammed behind Douglas.***

"What was that all about?" Lieutenant Miller asked.

My grandpa didn't answer him.

"Who do we have on duty tonight?" my grandpa asked.

"Reilly and I are on until ten o'clock, and then Benson and Moralesse have the night shift. Why?"

"I want someone out front twenty-four seven. No one comes up to this house without talking to you first, okay?"

"Okay," Miller said. "But do you want to tell me what's going on, boss? Why did you just blame Terri's murder on the CIA? Do you really think they were involved?"

"I honestly don't know what to think. I just know that Robert's dead and we don't have any answers. Until I get them, no one comes near Furious, you understand? No one."

"Sure, Bud," Miller replied.

"You call me on the radio before letting anyone near this house. And make sure it's Moralesse, not Benson, that relieves you at ten. I can't take chances with Benson. Not tonight. Not with something this important."

"Hey, Bud, you know I'm here for you. I'll do whatever you need."

"I know." My grandpa sighed.

Miller continued, "I'll stay on through the night shift and take up a position out front. I'll have Moralesse circling the block all night. You two get some rest, we've got it covered." Lieutenant Miller said as he turned around and walked out the back door.

I watched my grandpa walk over and lock the back door behind Miller.

"What's going on, Grandpa?"

"I don't know, Furious. And I don't want to scare you, but I figured we might as well be cautious. It can't hurt to have those guys out front. You'll be safe here."

"Safe from what? What's going on?"

My grandpa sighed. "Come over here and sit," he said, motioning toward the kitchen table. "I need to sit."

We sat down at the kitchen table and I could see Miller through the window. He was sitting in his dimly lit squad car in the driveway.

"Why did you say it was that Douglas guy's fault that my mom is dead?"

"He wasn't directly responsible," my grandpa said, "but I wouldn't say he's innocent, either."

"What do you mean? Someone is hunting down our family, aren't they?" I asked.

My grandpa looked shocked, and I was sure he was about to tell me that everything would be okay. That no one was hunting us.

But he didn't.

He looked me in the eyes and said, "Yes."

CHAPTER SIX

I *felt cold hearing the words come from his lips.*

"But why?" I begged my grandpa for answers. But he just stared at the kitchen floor. "Are we in danger, Grandpa?"

My grandpa looked at me a long time saying nothing.

"Am *I* in danger?" I asked.

"I think so," he finally said. "I think we both are. And I have no idea who to trust."

He rubbed his face with his giant hands. "Oh, Furious. I'm so sorry."

"Sorry? About what?"

My grandpa started to weep silently. "This is so far out of control. Your dad had a plan to keep you safe," he said with his face still in his hands. "He had a plan to get justice for your mom's death."

"What? What plan? What are you talking about?"

He rubbed his face one last time and turned toward me. His cheeks and eyes were red. "Your mom had a secret," he said. "She never wanted you to hear any of this. Heck, she never really told me much."

"What kind of secret?"

"Your dad came to me after the funeral. He told me about some bad guys who were after your mom. Your dad tried to help her. He reached out to some of his friends, powerful people. But they didn't help him."

"What people? What bad guys? What—" I suddenly realized I was yelling. I stopped and sat back in my chair.

"Please, Grandpa," I begged. "Please tell me what's going on."

"I guess it all started shortly after your mom got out of college," he said.

"Back in Minnesota," I offered.

"Right. Your dad got a job writing for a Saint Paul newspaper right after college, and your mom decided to stay with him in Minnesota. They got married shortly after graduation."

"Yeah," I said.

"Well, your mom had been a fantastic student. She majored in economics and Italian in school," my grandpa said.

"Yeah, I know."

My grandpa continued, "But what you don't know is shortly after your mom and dad were married, your mom was approached by Director Douglas."

"The CIA guy?" I asked.

"Yes. I guess Douglas had just been promoted to director of the international organized crime unit. He was putting together a new team of recruits and, somehow, he'd come across your mom."

"My mom? In the CIA?" I asked out loud. "What would the CIA want with Mom?"

"Well, Douglas was putting a team together to go after this really big Italian mob organization. I think her intelligence and knowledge of Italy and the language made her a natural for the job."

"My mom was in the CIA?"

"Yes," my grandpa replied.

"This is a joke, right? There is no way Mom was in the CIA. She was, like, some sort of accountant."

My grandpa didn't respond, but his expression didn't change. He was serious!

"That's like a page out of my dad's books," I said.

"Oh," my grandpa moaned, "you've got no idea."

"And you knew that she worked for the CIA? You knew this the entire time?" I asked.

"Yes, I knew. But she didn't talk about it much. I guess she couldn't really."

"So she lied to me this whole time? She lied about being an accountant? You all lied to me? I went around the world with her, thinking she was an accountant, but she was actually some sort of spy?"

I couldn't believe what I was hearing. Pictures of my mom flashed through my head. My mom leaving for work with her bags. My mom on the phone with work. With the CIA?

"What did she do for the CIA?" I asked. "I mean, if she wasn't an accountant? You said she was going after some Italian mob?"

My grandpa moaned again and rubbed his face hard this time.

"Grandpa?"

"I don't know any of this to be true. Like I said, your mom didn't tell me anything. She hadn't mentioned work in years. I just know what your dad told me."

"What did my dad tell you?"

"I wouldn't want you to think differently about—"

"What did he tell you?" I demanded.

"He said your mother was a CIA assassin."

CHAPTER SEVEN

My grandpa went on to tell me how, according to my dad, my mom was trained at some clandestine CIA assassin training facility called The Farm. And how she was assigned to monitor and kill key members in the Salvatore crime syndicate. My grandpa said the Salvatore crime syndicate was one of the world's largest criminal organizations and, according to my dad, my mom was starting to make an impact on the organization one leader at a time.

I just sat motionless. What do you say when you find out your mom was an assassin? What do you say when you discover your entire life was a lie—a lie that, apparently, everyone else was in on but you?

"How long had my dad known about this?" I asked.

"From the beginning," my grandpa said. "You might not like the next part, Furious," he warned.

Was he kidding? What could he tell me that would be more shocking than *Hey, did you know your mom was a highly trained government assassin?*

"Your dad," my grandpa continued. "A few years after joining the newspaper, he decided he would try to write books."

"I know," I said. "He published the first Carson Kidd book just before they got divorced."

My grandpa sat back in his chair and looked down at the floor. "That book caused the divorce."

"I know," I said. "My mom hated the fame and attention. She said my dad changed after the book came out."

"Yes, he did," my grandpa agreed. "But your dad wrote the book about your mom. The first book is almost word for word stories your mom had told your dad about the training at The Farm and her first mission."

"What?"

"Really," my grandpa said. "Your dad cried as he told me the story. Every Carson Kidd book had apparently been based on your mom's missions in their first six years of marriage."

"Are you saying that my mom was actually Carson Kidd?" I asked in disbelief.

My grandpa nodded. "Yes, I guess so."

"And my dad was a fraud?"

"No, Furious. Your dad wrote those books. They were just based on your mom's adventures."

"But they were my mom's stories. Not my dad's. And he had no right to tell them. Obviously, the fame and money meant more to him than his marriage. Or his own son."

My grandpa said nothing.

"Unbelievable. No wonder my mom hated those books and my dad's fame."

"Like I said, he regretted it in the end. And he was trying to do the right thing. Your dad loved you and your mom very much, and you need to know that he died trying to do the right thing."

"The right thing? Like what? Promoting yet another book? He was in town tonight promoting his latest book, Grandpa."

"You knew he was in town?"

"I went into the city to see him." Tears started to fall into my lap. "I saw him."

My grandpa didn't say anything.

"This guy just stood up in the crowd and started shooting."

The tears started falling faster, and my grandpa let out a heavy breath.

"That's what Douglas was talking about. He knew you were there tonight," my grandpa said.

"Yeah."

"This book was different, Furious," my grandpa said.

"Your dad's new book was his way of making up for everything. Unfortunately, I don't have a lot of the details, but I know your mom was really nervous about going to Galena. And I know she reached out to your dad before she left."

"I know. I gave her his latest cell phone number. I was shocked when she asked me for it. As far as I know, she had never called him. I knew something was wrong."

"Well, apparently they were sending her to Galena to go after some ultra-bad guy. The worst of the worst. Douglas had already sent in an agent who had failed. But, according to your dad, that agent might have actually been working for the Salvatores, too."

"Apparently my dad didn't try too hard to help. He didn't save her."

"Furious, I know this is hard to believe, but your dad loved your mom very much. I agree, he was selfish and made some bad—" My grandpa paused. "Some horrible decisions. But your mom did reach out to him, and he was trying to help her before she was killed. They had been in constant communication, and your dad went to Galena after your mom was killed. He made it his life's mission to investigate her murder himself."

"That's where he went after the funeral? That was the place that was too dangerous to take me? The reason he couldn't be with me?"

"Yeah," my grandpa said. "He felt awful about being away

from you. He truly did. But we both agreed it was safer for you to stay with me."

"Did he find anything?"

"Yeah, he did. Your dad used to be an amazing investigative journalist, you know?"

"Yeah, Mom told me. What did he find?"

"I don't know. I just know that he said the corruption was widespread. He said the Salvatore syndicate were known for their ability to penetrate every level of government. He had no idea where to turn or whom to trust. He reached out to some of his powerful friends, but no one would help him. Several of his buddies turned on him, even high up in the FBI and CIA. It seemed everyone was either working for or afraid of the Salvatores. So he decided to do what he had always done. He told your mom's story through Carson Kidd."

"The new book," I said, sitting up. "*Double Crossed*. It's about my mom's death?"

"Yes. He said the politicians couldn't ignore him once your mom's story was out in the open. He figured it was also the best way to keep you safe. His new book is the true story of your mom's death, the CIA corruption, and whatever the Salvatores were up to in Galena. He planned to go public with it in a big way next week. The entire world would know about your mom and the activities of the Salvatore crime syndicate."

"And they still will, right?" I asked.

My grandpa didn't respond.

"We can tell the world," I said. "We can tell them the story is real."

"I hope so," my grandpa answered.

CHAPTER EIGHT

I **was exhausted by the time I got up to my room. I'd** been living in my grandpa's guest bedroom for seven months. It was the longest I'd ever stayed in one place. But it had always felt temporary. I felt like a guest. I hadn't put anything on the walls or really settled in at all. I'd figured I would be moving to my dad's place in Minnesota at some point. It felt funny to walk into the room now, with the knowledge that this would be my home for the next several years. It looked so bare. I had some clothes in the closet and my phone. That was it. That was the extent of my worldly possessions.

I lay on the bed and searched the Internet for information on Carson Kidd, hoping to find out more about this entirely new side to my mom. A side I'd never known. And thanks to my dad's desire for fame and fortune, I was now able to read all about her day job. I was reading reviews of my dad's previous book, *Miss Fire*, when I must have dozed off. I don't know how long I was asleep, but it didn't take me long to wake up. I heard the floor creak and opened my eyes to the silhouette of a shotgun on my ceiling.

"Whoa!" My heart raced as I sat up in the bed.

"Shhh," my grandpa whispered. "Stay down."

My eyes tried to focus as I pushed the hair away from them. It took a few seconds to grasp what was going on, and then I started to make out the shape of my grandpa standing next to my window with a shotgun over his shoulder.

"What's going on?" I whispered.

"It's Miller. He's not picking up the radio. None of them are."

"Is his car still out there?" I asked as I walked toward him. My heart was pounding hard. It felt like it would come right through my chest. I was sure my grandpa could hear it.

"I can't tell. It looks like someone might be in the car."

"Maybe they all fell asleep," I suggested.

"Well, that wouldn't be the first time," my grandpa said as he started walking toward the door.

"What are you doing?"

"I'm going out there," he said. "You stay put and stay away from the window."

"What if someone is out there? What if those Salvatore people are here?"

My grandpa racked the slide on the shotgun and loaded a shell into the barrel. "Well, I'd hate to be them. I'll be fine, Furious. Just sit tight."

"Please," I begged like a little kid. "Please just call the police, Grandpa."

"I *am* the police," he said as he slipped out of my room.

I sat on the floor and held my breath as I listened to him walking down the stairwell. And then there was silence. Five minutes passed with nothing but the sound of my heart pounding. Ten minutes. Fifteen. I could feel panic sweeping over me as I inched toward the window. I got to my knees and looked out onto the driveway. Miller's squad car was still running, but it was too dark to see inside it. And there was no sign of my grandpa anywhere.

I thought I heard something coming from the hallway, but it was hard to be sure. The sound of my thumping heart now made it nearly impossible to hear anything. I took a couple of deep breaths and called out into the dark.

"Grandpa? Is that you?"

Nothing.

Then I thought I heard a noise coming from the driveway. I looked out the window. Miller's driver's-side door was open. It was dark, but it looked like my grandpa was leaning into the squad. Maybe he was using the radio? Or maybe

Miller was still in the car. I took several deep breaths and watched as my grandpa continued to lean into the squad car. Then the dome light came on and I could see my grandpa's face. It was inches from Lieutenant Miller's. Miller looked lifeless. I was about to stand up and go help my grandpa when a pair of bright lights suddenly lit the entire vehicle. A dark sedan pulled up inches from the back of Miller's squad car. Maybe it was Moralesse. The car easily could have been an unmarked cop car. But now I could make out the silhouette of two people inside.

A large man in a long leather trench coat got out of the sedan's passenger side and started slowly walking between his car and Miller's squad. I saw the reflection of a knife in his hand as he stepped into the beam from his headlights. I looked back at my grandpa. He was out of the car and on his knees. He looked like he was fumbling with something on the ground.

"GET UP!" I yelled. "GET UP!"

As my grandpa turned to look at me, I could see it was Miller that he was fumbling with. Miller was bleeding on the ground in front of him. My grandpa was trying to stop the bleeding. I pointed frantically to the car in the driveway, but the guy in the trench coat was nowhere to be seen. And then the driveway went dark as the sedan's headlights shut off.

Where did the man in the trench coat go? I pounded on the window as the driver of the sedan slowly got out. I needed to warn my grandpa that there were two men.

My grandpa picked up the shotgun at his side and stood up. He began to point it toward the driver. That's when I saw the man in the trench coat reappear. He had circled around Miller's squad and was now walking up behind my grandpa. I screamed and pounded on the window. But it was too late. The man in the trench coat slid the knife across my grandpa's throat, and my grandpa dropped to the ground.

Then the two men looked up at me.

CHAPTER NINE

I **turned and ran toward the stairs. My legs felt like**
they were in quicksand. I tried to move fast. I tried to focus
on each step but couldn't. I missed one of the stairs with my
left foot and tumbled to the bottom.

Oh, god! Get up! Get up!

I reached out, grabbed the end of the railing, and pulled
myself up. Time seemed to slow again. Just like it had in the
ballroom. I stood at the bottom of the stairs, not knowing
what to do.

*Where are they now? Are they in the house? Can I
hide?*

I walked down the hall, into the kitchen. The back door
was wide open.

I felt sick. I didn't want to die. I didn't have the guts to go through the open door.

I sank to the floor next to the sink. I needed a weapon. I needed to protect myself. I fumbled through the cupboard under the sink and found cleaners, tools, and old cookie tins. I opened one of the tins hoping to find one of my grandpa's guns. There was no gun. The tin was full of cash. I grabbed a fistful of money, shoved it in my pocket, and then grabbed a bottle of Raid. Maybe I could run out of the door spraying the Raid? Maybe it would blind them?

I inched toward the open door trying desperately to hear something, anything, other than the thumping of my heart. I put my finger on the top of the bottle and prepared to spray.

On three!

Come on, Furious, you can do this!

Get ready.

Get set.

But I couldn't move. They were there. They had to be there. This was suicide for sure. Bug spray? Against killers?

I started to cry. I was stuck. There was nothing I could do.

I stepped back toward the sink. Toward the microwave.

The microwave. I could use the microwave. Maybe I could distract them and get out.

I opened the microwave, placed the bottle of Raid in it, pushed 2:22, and hit start. The metal bottle started to spark immediately, and I ran back down the hallway to my grandpa's den. I unlocked the window in the corner of the room and crouched down in the dark. I couldn't hear anything over the thumping in my ears, but I could already smell the pesticide. And then there was a sudden flash of light and a huge explosion.

The bright-white light dimmed to an orange glow, and smoke started to fill the den. I stood to open the window. I dove out headfirst and landed on the little service sidewalk that ran between my grandpa's house and the McMahons'. I thought briefly about pounding on Andy's door but decided it was best to keep moving. I ran through the McMahons' backyard and jumped the fence into the Gunneruds' yard. I continued to cut through backyards until I got to the train station. The first train out of New Canaan left at 5:30 a.m. I pulled out my phone. I had an hour to wait. I walked across the street to a small park and sat behind a bush.

CHAPTER TEN

I *sat in the bushes for the better part of an hour, lis-*tening to what sounded like dozens of fire trucks racing to my grandpa's house. Then I used some of my grandpa's money to get on the train and head toward New York. I figured I was safest riding the subway around New York for a couple of hours while I figured out what to do. I needed to get help but had no idea who to trust. If I went to the police, I was afraid that the CIA would find out. And Director Douglas and the CIA were probably higher up the food chain than the police when it came to crimes. What if they handed me over to Douglas? My grandpa didn't trust Douglas, and neither did I. Maybe he was in on my mom's murder. And my dad's and grandpa's. Maybe he was working for the Salvatores.

I finally got off the train at Grand Central station and sat down on a bench in the main terminal, next to a guy who looked like he probably ran some big bank or something. He was reading the *New York Times*. Dad's face was taking up most of the front page, and my grandpa's would probably be on there tomorrow. I hung my head in my lap and tried not to cry. I loved my grandpa. He was a good guy. A great guy. And he died trying to protect me.

I sat on the bench staring at the crowd. All of these people had someone. Friends. Family. People in their life. I had no one. They were all gone. All killed. I was absolutely alone on the planet. I breathed deep and stared. I tried to think of someone I could trust.

The banker man got up after twenty minutes and left his paper on the bench. I picked it up. The front page featured a picture of my dad that I had never seen. He was wearing some sort of hunting jacket with a leather patch on the shoulder. He looked like he was on a safari. Maybe in Africa. Man, he was so tough. I never would've imagined anything could have hurt him. I stared at the photo and thought about life without him. All the little things we'd never get to do together. All the conversations we'd never have.

I wiped my eyes and thumbed through the paper, looking for more photos of my dad. There were several articles about him. One was an in-depth obituary chronicling his life. There was a long story detailing his murder, and a short interview about his yet-to-be-released book *Double Crossed*.

I read the interview:

Double Crossed, the sixth installment in the series about hard-hitting CIA agent Carson Kidd becomes available next Thursday. Below are excerpts from an interview with Robert Jones about the book, his life, and his preparations for its sale.

REPORTER: Your books have become wildly popular. Worldwide, you sell something like one book every minute of the day. That's astonishing!

JONES: Yeah, I've heard that number before.

REPORTER: What do you make of that?

JONES: What do I make of it? Well, it's great. I'm incredibly grateful to all the Kidd fans. We're having a good time together.

REPORTER: The sixth book is coming out in a week, and you and/or your publisher insist on keeping incredible security surrounding the book, right?

JONES: That's right.

REPORTER: Why the secrecy, Robert?

JONES: This book is very different from all the others. I'm certain when this is all said and done, everyone will understand the unique situation driving the unique launch.

REPORTER: Yes, I'm glad you said it. The circumstances have been unorthodox, to say the least. I understand you wrote this book in a very short period of time and pushed your publisher hard for a quick release.

JONES: That's right.

REPORTER: Why the urgency with this book?

JONES: What do you mean?

REPORTER: I mean, I've heard reports that you wrote this book in about a month and insisted on a previously unheard-of publication schedule. Why the rush?

JONES: Like I said, a lot of this will make sense after the release. There is nothing traditional or normal about this Kidd book.

REPORTER: Robert, don't you find all of this a bit ridiculous? A little over the top?

JONES: No, not at all.

REPORTER: Is it just a marketing ploy?

JONES: Not at all. This is real. This is real life. This book, more than any of my previous books, is real life. You understand that? People's lives are at stake. You need to understand that.

REPORTER: What do you mean, "Lives are at stake"?

JONES: There are many people counting on me to tell the story.

REPORTER: That's true, you do have a massive

fan base. Are you at all worried that in your rush to publish this book that you might not have taken the care you took with the previous Kidd books?

JONES: No.

REPORTER: Are there more Carson Kidd books in your future? This isn't the end of the series, is it? You don't kill off Carson Kidd?

JONES: I don't kill him. But that doesn't mean he's not dead.

REPORTER: Well, that kind of leads me to my next question. Let's talk about the title. The new book is titled *Double Crossed*.

JONES: That's right.

REPORTER: What can you tell us about the title? What does "double crossed" refer to?

JONES: I think the title speaks for itself. It's about betrayal. Betrayal of trust.

REPORTER: Can you tell us more?

JONES: You'll have to read it with everyone else next Thursday.

REPORTER: Why release the book on a Thursday? As you know, most books come out on Tuesdays.

JONES: I was told that was the soonest they could get the books out.

REPORTER: Okay, one final question. Is this book dedicated to anyone?

JONES: This one is dedicated to my son, Furious, and my agent, Sloan Harrison. Sloan has always stood by my side. And he moved mountains to help me pull off this new book. We were set to publish a different book, but he knew how important this project was to me.

I closed the paper. Sloan Harrison was my dad's agent, and his best friend, too. I hadn't seen Sloan since my mom's funeral. My dad and Sloan had been best friends since they were kids back in Minnesota. They were best men at each other's weddings. And Sloan was my godfather. My mother never liked Sloan, but she always said he was the brain behind my father's success. And no matter where we were in the world, Sloan had always found a way to send me a present on my birthday. Always.

I turned my phone back on and searched for my dad's website. I clicked Contact Us, and Sloan's office address and phone number came up on the screen. Maybe Sloan could help. Sloan had to know about the book being real and about my mom's murder. He was a successful, powerful guy, and the closest thing I had left to a relative—maybe he could help.

I needed to talk to Sloan.

I used some more of my grandpa's money to take a cab uptown to Sloan's office. The security guard stopped me in the lobby.

"May I help you?"

"I'm here to see Sloan Harrison from Harrison, Smythe, and Moore."

"Do you have an appointment?" he asked.

"No. But I think he'll see me. I'm Furious Jones. Robert Jones's son."

He looked shocked. Or concerned. He either knew my dad or was reacting to my stupid name.

"Ah, hang on just one minute," he said and picked up the phone. I couldn't hear his conversation, but it was brief.

"I'm so sorry for your loss. Please take the elevator to the fifteenth floor. Kristyn . . . ah . . . Mr. Harrison's assistant will help you."

"Thank you," I replied.

He pushed a button under the counter, and I walked through the turnstile to the bank of elevators. I stepped into an open elevator and punched 15. I stepped out into a lavish mahogany-paneled lobby. Kristyn was waiting for me. And so was Director Douglas.

CHAPTER ELEVEN

Hello again, Furious," Douglas said.

Douglas? What was he doing here?

"Hi, Furious, my name is Kristyn. I was one of Mr. Harrison's assistants." She stuck her hand out and I shook it.

"We're all so sorry for the loss of your—" She started crying before she could finish. This was a mistake.

"You'll have to excuse Kristyn," Douglas said. "These guys have had a rough couple of days."

You've got to be kidding me. They've *had a rough couple of days?*

I looked around the lobby. There was a woman sitting behind the desk and six or seven uniformed cops standing in the lobby talking to one another. They were clearly pulling out all the stops for my dad.

"I stopped by to talk to Sloan. Is he around?" I asked.

"I'm glad you're here, Furious. Let's find a place to talk." Douglas stepped aside and gestured down the hallway. "Kristyn, is there some place Furious and I can talk in private?"

"Sure," Kristyn replied. "You can use the conference room. Follow me." "Where's Sloan?" I asked again.

"Mr. Harrison is dead," Douglas said as he put his hand on my shoulder and started guiding me down the hall.

Dead? Did he say dead?

As I tried to process what he'd just told me, Douglas and I followed Kristyn down a long hallway with offices on both sides. They were mostly empty. But I could hear voices and noises from an office on the right. There was a cop standing in the doorway. The voices grew louder.

"Don't look," Douglas said.

But it was too late. I'd already looked. And I saw Sloan's body on the floor of his office. I looked away, but the snapshot was already there. Etched in my mind. And it would be there forever.

We kept walking, and I didn't say anything. Sloan was truly the last person I could count on to help me and now he was dead. Gone. Clearly these guys could get to anyone. Were they killing everyone who knew my dad's new book was a true story? As far as I knew, I was the last one on the list.

The last living person to know that whatever was happening in Galena, Illinois, was nonfiction. If they killed me, it would stop here. The book would come out next Thursday, and the world would assume that it was just a fictional story. Like they had assumed with all the previous Kidd books. And the Salvatore crime syndicate, and whoever else, would get away with murder. Or, more accurately, *murders*.

Kristyn led us to a large glass-walled conference room at the end of the hall. I noticed an EXIT sign above a door next to the conference room. Maybe I'd get a chance to run. My grandpa thought Douglas might be mixed up in my mom's death, and my dad had made it clear that the Salvatores had infiltrated the CIA, so I couldn't trust Douglas. Or anyone in the CIA.

"In here," Kristyn said, motioning with her left hand.

I circled around the large conference-room table. I wanted to sit as far away from Douglas as I could. A wall at the far end of the room was lined with dozens of books, carefully lit and displayed on glass shelves. Most of them were my dad's.

I walked up and grabbed a copy of *Miss Fire*, my dad's fifth book. The one I had read so many great reviews about.

"I hear this is the best one in the series," I said.

"Yes, it's very popular. But I guess they're all popular," Kristyn said with a smile.

I looked at the cover. It had a silhouette of a man in the

foreground looking at the Eiffel Tower. I wondered what adventure my mom went on in this book. I knew my mom could speak a little French. She could actually speak several languages in addition to Italian. I guess now I knew why. And my mom and I had spent a couple of months in Paris about a year and a half ago. Was she there killing people? I wondered.

There was a sticker on the cover that said GET A SNEAK PEEK AT *DOUBLE CROSSED*.

"What's this sticker?" I asked Kristyn.

"Oh, that was the publisher's idea. They placed those stickers on his other books. There is a code on the back of the sticker that allows you to get excerpts leading up to the book's launch next Thursday. Can I get either of you something to eat or drink?"

I hadn't thought of it until she mentioned food, but I was starving. I hadn't eaten since late yesterday afternoon.

"I'd love something to eat, if it isn't too much trouble," I said.

"Oh, no trouble at all. Do you like scones? There's a coffee shop downstairs, and they make killer sco—" She paused halfway through the word "scone," and her cheeks reddened. "They make great scones," she finished.

"That would be great," I said.

"Anything for you?" she asked, turning toward Douglas.

"No, I'm fine, thank you."

Kristyn left the room and Douglas turned toward me.

"What brings you here today, Furious?" Douglas asked as he sat down across from me.

"I was just coming to see Sloan."

"What for?"

"Just to talk, I guess."

"Do you two talk a lot? Were you close?" Douglas asked.

"Sort of," I lied. He was my godfather, but we weren't particularly close.

"Oh," Douglas dropped his voice to a whisper. "I'm sorry, I didn't know that."

It was strange. This didn't seem like the same guy who'd stood in my grandpa's kitchen yesterday yelling. He seemed kind. Trusting. I wondered if that was all part of the plan. Kind of a good cop, bad cop thing.

"You know I was friends with your mother?"

His voice went up an octave at the end of the sentence. Like it was more of a question than a statement. I didn't respond.

"Did your grandpa tell you about me?"

"No," I lied.

"Were you at your dad's talk the other night? The night he was killed?"

"Yes."

"So you're not going to lie to me about *everything*, then?" Douglas said, leaning back in his chair.

How did he know I lied about my grandpa telling me who he was? Was my grandpa's house bugged?

"Did you sit with Attorney General Como at the event?"

"Yes," I said.

"How well do you know Joe Como?" Douglas asked.

"Not at all. I just met him that night."

"Did he approach you? How did you end up sitting together?"

"We kind of bumped into each other," I said.

"What did you talk about?"

"Not much," I said.

Douglas didn't respond. He just stared at me for several long seconds.

"Believe it or not, Furious, I cared about your mother, and I care about you."

I said nothing.

"I have reason to believe you're in serious danger," Douglas said.

"You think?" I asked. "My mom, dad, and grandpa have all been murdered. I'd say it's fair to assume I'm in a little danger."

"Your grandpa?" Douglas sat up. "What are you talking about?"

I suddenly remembered I needed to be careful. My grandpa didn't trust Douglas. And he seemed to think he might have even had a hand in my parents' deaths. I couldn't trust him. I couldn't trust anyone.

"What happened to your grandpa?" Douglas asked again.

I could feel my eyes watering as I sat looking across the table. God, I had no one.

Douglas pulled out his cell phone and, without saying a word, walked out of the room. This was my chance. If I was going to get away, I had to go now.

CHAPTER TWELVE

I *couldn't sit around here and wait to see if my grandpa* was right or not about not trusting Douglas. Clearly Douglas had been unable to save my mom from whatever had happened in Galena, so how would he save me? No, I needed to go. I needed to find some facts and figure out what was going on.

I stuck my head out into the hallway and Douglas was standing about five feet from the conference room door. He was on his phone and facing away from me. I looked at the exit next to me. It was two feet away, but Douglas would surely hear the door. I needed a distraction. I needed Douglas to move.

I had absolutely nothing left to lose, so I pulled out my

phone and tapped the Internet icon. My browser was still on my dad's contact page. I clicked on Sloan's phone number and stepped back into the conference room. A woman answered.

"Harrison, Smythe, and Moore, how may I direct your call?" the woman asked.

I spoke softly into the phone, "Director Douglas, please."

There was a short pause and then she put me on hold. I lowered the phone to my side and stood near the door. A minute later I heard a woman's voice in the hallway. And then the deep rumble of Douglas's voice. Then silence. Seconds later I heard Douglas's voice coming from my phone.

"Hello. Hello? Who's there?"

I clicked cancel, shoved the phone into my pocket, and opened the door.

"Oh, hello." A tall brunette was standing directly in front of me. She was probably the woman who had answered the phone. "Agent Douglas will be right back."

"Tell him I'll meet him in the lobby," I said as I pushed the exit door open.

"Ah, no! Wait, I—"

I didn't bother with the rest of her protest. I stepped into the stairwell, grabbed the metal railing, and started moving quickly down the stairs.

This was crazy. There was no way this would work.

I started taking two steps at a time. Then I started jumping the last several stairs at each landing. There was a landing at each floor and halfway between each floor. That meant I had to clear thirty landings to get to the bottom. To get free.

How many had I passed so far? Three? Maybe four? I tried to move faster. The entire staircase was made of metal. Like one big metal structure sitting inside a giant concrete shaft. It was loud. The noise from my jumping echoed in the shaft. I'd never hear Douglas coming after me. He was sure to have hung up by now. Was he already on the stairs?

Go! Go! Move! Move!

I was flying down the stairs. I was in a rhythm. My breathing was getting loud. I was sure the entire building could hear me now. My legs were burning. My right thigh felt odd. Like it was pulsing. Or twitching. I stopped to catch my breath. I was breathing hard. I bent over the railing and looked up toward the fifteenth floor. Then I felt the twitch again. It was my phone. It was vibrating in my pocket. I pulled it out. The screen said I had an incoming call from the Harrison, Smythe, and Moore agency.

Shoot! Caller ID. I really hadn't thought this through. Could he track me? Could he track my phone? Isn't that what the CIA did? I hit ignore, shoved the phone back in my pocket, and continued down the stairs. I gripped the railing hard at each landing and flung myself around the corners. The eleven floor. Tenth floor. Ninth. I kept going. I hit the sixth-floor landing and thought I heard someone enter the stairwell. I stopped and tried to listen. My heart was throbbing in my ears. I breathed in deep and held my breath. Someone was definitely coming down the stairs. I started moving fast. A head start was all I had. I was jumping three stairs with every move now. I imagined Douglas was too.

Five. Four. Three. I kept moving. Kept jumping. Two. One. I stopped and took a couple of deep breaths before opening the first-floor door. Someone was definitely moving quickly down the stairs. There was no doubt about it—Douglas was close.

I pushed the door open and walked out into the corridor near the bank of elevators. I wiped the sweat from my forehead and walked toward the main set of doors. I walked past the security guard and gave him a nod. I was twenty feet from the door. Fifteen feet. Ten. Five. Then I heard my name.

"Furious?"

I kept walking.

"Furious?"

It sounded more like a question than a statement. I recognized the voice. It was Kristyn. I didn't look back. I just kept walking. I pushed myself into the revolving door and looked over my shoulder as it turned. Kristyn was standing in the lobby, holding a bag of pastries. My scones.

CHAPTER THIRTEEN

I*thought about heading to the subway, but where* would I go? I couldn't go back to my grandpa's house. Obviously it wasn't safe and, judging from the number of fire trucks that had rolled through the streets of New Canaan, my grandpa's house must have burned to the ground.

I needed to know what was going on. Why was the Salvatore crime syndicate killing my family? I needed to know what was in my dad's new book. What had my mom discovered in Galena? I thought of my mom as Carson Kidd. And then I thought of the sticker and the code on my dad's latest book. Kristyn had said it unlocked a couple of excerpts of the new book. Maybe there would be enough information to give me a better idea of what was going on in Galena. I searched my phone for a bookstore. The closest one was five blocks away. I started to run.

It wasn't hard to find my dad's books in the store. They were piled a hundred high as you walked in. The store seemed to be preparing for the excitement surrounding my dad's new book. His death was sure to bring more publicity too. Lots more.

I grabbed a copy of his fifth book, *Miss Fire*, and headed to the café. I purchased a Coke, a scone, and the book. I handed the cashier some more of my grandpa's cash and felt bad as I looked down at the photo of my dad on the back of the book. I had never really gotten to know him. I'd always figured that we would spend time together later. I'd figured we'd make up for the lost years. But now that was impossible. And now I'd found out I didn't really know my mom, either. Not really.

I sat down and peeled back the sticker on the front of the book to reveal a seven-digit code along with instructions to enter the code at CarsonKidd.com. I pulled my phone out and started to type in the website when the phone began to vibrate.

It was an incoming call from a private number.

I pushed talk.

"Do you seriously think you can run from the CIA?" It was Douglas.

CHAPTER FOURTEEN

Douglas was right—what was I thinking? This was the CIA. The most secretive and powerful government entity on the planet. And Douglas had my phone number. He could easily have my phone tracked. He knew exactly where I was, and I'm sure he was only a block or two away.

I stood up to go. I could throw my phone in the trash and Douglas wouldn't be able to track me, but where would I go?

I picked up my book and food and walked over to the trash. I was about to toss my phone in with my Coke and half-eaten scone when I realized what I had to do.

I had to go to Galena. I had nothing left in my life and nothing left to lose. I had to figure out what was going on there. Maybe I could get some proof that my mom was murdered by the Salvatore crime syndicate. Maybe I could get proof that my dad's new book was a factual recounting of . . . of whatever.

I searched buses and trains from New York to Galena on my phone. It looked like the Greyhound bus was my best bet. The ticket cost $169. I hadn't counted my grandpa's cash, but I knew there were at least several hundred dollars in my pocket. I guessed that would be enough to get there and, and then . . . I don't know.

I looked at the clock on my phone. It was just after four o'clock. The bus to Galena left in fifty-six minutes. The Greyhound station was across town. I needed to hurry. I threw my phone in the trash, left the bookstore, and started running.

CHAPTER FIFTEEN

I *got to the bus station with four minutes to spare. The* bus was nice. Not first-class Singapore Airlines nice, but still nice. It had comfortable seats, Wi-Fi, and outlets built into each row. Not that it mattered. I was phone-less. But it wasn't a total loss. The bus had over a dozen high school girls on it, and the pretty blonde across the aisle kept looking over at me. She clearly had no idea just how young I was. Aside from the Greyhound ticket agent assuming I was older than I was, talking to high school girls might have been the only other advantage of being six four in middle school.

"Where are you headed?" I asked.

"Northwestern in Chicago. We're going on a school trip." She smiled. "Northwestern has the top journalism school in the country, and we all work for our school newspaper on the East Coast."

"What school do you go to?"

"Watercrest Academy," she said.

"Watercrest? That's the all-girl boarding school in Westport, Connecticut, right?"

"Yes, how do you know about Watercrest?" she asked.

"I make it a point to know the locations of all the all-girl schools on the East Coast," I said.

"Oh, really?" She smiled.

"No." I smiled back. "Not really."

"How about you? Where are you headed?"

"I'm going to upstate Illinois. A little town called Galena," I replied.

She lit up a little. "I love Galena. I was just there last summer for the hot air balloon races. It's beautiful. Have you been there before?"

"Nope. First time. But I've heard it's nice," I lied. I had never heard a thing about Galena. "My name is Furious." I extended my hand across the aisle and winced a little. Should I have given her my real name? What if she posted it online? *I met the cutest guy named Furious on the bus just now. And he's headed to Galena.* The CIA would be sure to pick that up with all of their electronic spy equipment.

But now she was wearing the same look that everyone wore when I gave my name.

"*Furious?* What kind of name is *Furious?*" she asked.

"Yes, that is the question." I paused. "I think my parents were either attempting to create a professional athlete, build character, or just really thought it would be funny to inflict me with this name. I imagine it'll be a self-fulfilling prophecy someday."

"A prophecy?" she asked.

"Yeah. I'm bound to be unbelievably furious after a life-time with this name."

She smiled. "Why don't you ask them why they chose it?"

"Well, my mom always told me a story about me hitting the doctor in the nose when I was born, but I suspect she just made it up," I said.

"Why don't you ask her?"

"I can't; my mom and dad are both dead." Wow, that was the first time I'd ever said that.

She gave me a kind, long, sympathetic smile. "I'm sorry to hear that," she said. "And actually, I like your name. Mine's Emma."

"Emma? Whoa, now, that is an unusual name, isn't it? That must have been quite the cross to bear growing up. How did you ever cope with such an unusual name? I can't even imagine the trouble a name like Emma would've created for you."

She continued to smile. She had a great smile.

"Well, Emma, any recommendations on what I should

do in Galena? Since you've been there and all."

"There's actually a lot to do. They have great canoeing, hiking, and shopping. I went with my boyfriend's family last summer. His parents live in Chicago and have a place at this huge resort just outside of Galena. And we spent a lot of time at Ulysses S. Grant's house. My boyfriend knows a ton about history and stuff. He goes to Yale."

So not only was she too old for me, she had a college boyfriend, too. This girl was way out of my league.

"Lucky him." I paused and smiled. "Yale is a great school. So are your parents okay with you dating a college guy? Maybe you should seriously consider dating someone younger?"

"No, they're cool with it. They like Andrew, and they know that high school guys can be so immature." Then she quickly added, "No offense, though."

None taken, I thought. *I'm two years away from high school.*

"So, Northwestern. You want to be a journalist? Are you thinking of going to Northwestern after high school?"

"Maybe," she said. "Or I might look at Columbia. You know, to stay closer to Andrew."

"You look like a journalist," I replied.

"How do you look like a journalist? Curious? Inquisitive?"

"Patient," I replied.

She smiled.

"Patient enough to hang in there and watch newspapers be replaced by the Internet," I added.

"Ah, you're one of those?" she responded, the smile now gone.

"Realistic about the future of newspapers?" I asked. "I mean, the day of the newspaper is gone. It's dead. No one reads the newspaper anymore."

"No," she replied, "I meant that you must be one of those naïve people who refuses to realize that no matter the medium, it is the content that matters. It is the research skills and the craft. That will never change. It will dress differently and take different forms. But the craft will always be just that—a craft."

Now I smiled. "You're right."

"Of course I am," she replied as her phone rang.

I looked out the window as she answered her phone. It was probably the Yale man.

CHAPTER SIXTEEN

I *figured there was no way Douglas and the CIA could* track me now. I had no phone, no electronic devices, no credit cards. I had nothing to track, and I paid for my ticket in cash. After all the taxes and fees, I was left with just over $300. It wasn't going to get me very far—but I was alive and safe, for the moment.

The bus went dark as we entered the Lincoln Tunnel. Cars were shooting by just inches from the bus. You've got to love New Yorkers. I wondered when I'd see New York again.

"So why Galena?" Emma was off the phone.

"Sightseeing, I guess. My family has connections there and I thought I'd check it out."

"You'll love it. Oh—" She suddenly bounced a little in

her seat and spun toward me. "Make sure to check out The Atomic Toy Company on Main Street. They've got these awesome old toys. And the candy shop. It's a serious old-school candy store. The owner's family invented this candy called Chuckles or something. Anyways, they're awesome."

"Okay. Toys and candy—check."

"Where are you staying?" Emma asked.

Good question, I thought. I had no idea. With three hundred bucks, I was probably staying in a cornfield.

"Somewhere cheap," I replied.

"We stayed at this quaint little inn on top of the bluff overlooking the town."

"I'm not sure I can afford 'quaint.'"

"No, it really wasn't much. You don't get breakfast there, like at a B&B, but this cute old lady owns it. I think she just likes having people around."

"Well, then quaint might be in my future."

"But don't hold me to it. It could be more now. Galena gets busy this time of year with all the Chicago tourists checking out the fall leaves."

"Cool. The inn on the bluff, I'll check it out."

"I think it was called Betty's Inn or Betty's Manor or something," Emma said as she pulled a laptop out of her bag. "Here, I'll look it up for you."

She clicked around for a few minutes and found Betty's Bluff Inn. She said they were running a fall colors special. If

I didn't eat a thing, I'd have enough for four or five nights. Great.

"Are you from the Midwest?" I asked.

"No. I grew up in Oregon. But my mom and dad live in California now. How about you?"

"I kind of grew up everywhere, sort of like an army brat."

"Where do you live now?" she asked.

Right here on this bus, I thought. "I was living in New Canaan, Connecticut, until recently," I replied.

"Nice."

"It's okay."

She closed her laptop and slipped it back in her bag.

"Can I ask a huge favor?" I said.

"Sure."

"Can I borrow your laptop real quick? They're offering a sneak peek at this new book, and I'm dying to read it," I said, holding up my dad's book.

"Oh, I love Robert Jones. Is it a chapter from his book that comes out next week?" she asked.

"Yes."

"Then yes, you can use my computer, but only if I can read the chapter when you're done." Then she added, "It's sad what happened to him."

"Yeah," I agreed. "It is."

I pulled up my dad's website, entered the code, and found one excerpt available for download. There was a counter that indicated additional excerpts would be available in twenty hours. I read the first excerpt.

The Central Intelligence Agency, better known as the CIA, was headquartered in Langley, Virginia. Not too far from the CIA's assassin training grounds, called The Farm. Carson Kidd had fond memories of being trained at The Farm.

The CIA had recruited Kidd right out of college. Kidd had studied economics and foreign languages in school—two skill sets the CIA treasured dearly.

Kidd entered the CIA a naïve intellectual type but, after nine long months at The Farm, the CIA had turned him into one of the most elite and deadly killing machines on the planet. Kidd was equally equipped to kill someone at one thousand yards with a high-powered sniper rifle as he was to kill someone three feet away with his bare hands. And that was actually what he wanted to do today. He wanted to kill someone for summoning him back to Langley. He hated coming to CIA headquarters. It was full of executive pencil-pushing types. Men and women who had either never been in the field as active spies or, as in Kidd's case, an assassin. Or if they had been spies and killers, it had been many years ago. And now they all sat behind desks, getting fat and telling other people what to do. Kidd hated desks and, more than anything, Kidd hated being told what to do.

He squeezed his fists tight as he walked up to his boss's office, deep inside the Langley building. He pushed the door open and walked in without knocking.

"Well, it's good to see you too," Kidd's boss, Director Douglas, said as he stood up from behind his desk. "Come on in. Don't bother knocking or anything."

David Douglas had been the Director of International Organized Crime for over six years and he had personally recruited and trained Carson Kidd.

Shortly after being named Director of International Organized Crime, Douglas realized that the Salvatore crime syndicate had penetrated most of the world's government organizations, including the CIA. The Salvatore crime syndicate was based in Sicily but had a large and vast network that covered most of the globe. It was far and away the most brutal Mafia organization in the world, and Douglas knew that if he was to have any chance at taking on such a powerful organization, he would need to build an elite force of killers from the ground up. A group that was free from corruption. A group that could kill the world's top killers and then disappear into the shadows.

Douglas personally put his recruits through the CIA's brutal assassin training program. Douglas's team had been given black operation status. The black ops designation gave them freedom to operate without having to report to anyone inside the CIA. Technically speaking, black operations didn't exist. They didn't appear on any budget or spreadsheet. Nor did the people that work them. They were ghosts. They were set loose to accomplish their missions by whatever means necessary. The only real rule that applied to the CIA black ops programs was they were only allowed to operate outside the United States. All internal operations inside US borders belonged to the FBI. At least on paper.

"What am I doing here, Douglas?" Kidd demanded. "You know I hate coming here."

"Carson, I'd like you to meet John Gibson." Douglas motioned to a man sitting in a leather chair in the corner of the room.

Gibson didn't get up, and Kidd didn't acknowledge the man's existence. He just continued to look at Douglas.

"What am I doing here?" he demanded again.

"Have a seat, Carson." Douglas motioned to a chair directly in front of Douglas's desk.

Carson picked up the chair and repositioned it so he could see Douglas, Gibson, and the door. Some habits died hard.

"Okay," he said, sitting down. "Now are you going to tell me why you pulled me out of France?"

Douglas sighed and pursed his lips tight. Kidd could tell this was going to be bad news.

"What?" Kidd insisted.

"Mr. Gibson is my counterpart at the FBI. He heads up their organized crime program here in the states," Douglas said.

Kidd looked at Gibson. The FBI was at Langley? That was one for the books.

"What?" Kidd asked. "Are you here for some pointers? Want some trade craft advice from the pros, do you?"

"Funny," Gibson said.

Douglas interjected before Kidd got too fired up. "They're our friends, Carson. Let's try and remember we're all on the same side." Douglas paused, pushed his chin down a little, and looked at Kidd for a sign that he understood.

"Okay," Kidd said. "Right. We're all one big happy family."

"We've got a situation here," Douglas continued. "It's pretty bad."

Kidd could now tell that Douglas was serious. That something was truly wrong.

"What's going on?"

Gibson got up, walked over to Douglas's desk, and sat on the corner. "As you know, the Salvatore crime syndicate has had a major operation in Chicago for years."

"Yeah," Kidd said, wondering what in the world this had to do with him. It would be illegal for the CIA to do anything about the Salvatore syndicate in Chicago. That was clearly FBI territory.

"Well," Gibson continued, "my team has had a pretty good track record of infiltrating them."

"Okay," Kidd said impatiently.

Douglas must have seen that Kidd was growing restless, so he jumped in.

"The FBI was doing a stellar job until a local Chicago woman named Jensen got in the way," Douglas offered.

"Got in the way how?" Kidd asked.

"Jensen took over the local gang task force in Chicago," Gibson said.

"At the city level," Douglas added.

"Right," Gibson continued, "and she has been cutting very aggressive deals with all of the Salvatore scumbags. She's offering up sweet cash rewards and witness protection plans to anyone who is willing to rat out other Salvatore scumbags. She's cut over forty deals this year. Many of them with stone-cold killers."

"So she's giving these murderous thugs a pile of cash, a new identity, and moving them to some secret location where they get to live out the rest of their miserable lives in comfort," Kidd said, "instead of rotting in some jail cell?"

"Yes. She's moving the mobsters and their families," Gibson said. "She's moved over two hundred people so far."

"Our taxes at work," Kidd commented.

"Not ours," Douglas corrected. "This is a state-run witness protection program. Not federal."

"A state-run program?" Kidd asked. "I've never heard of such a thing."

"Illinois is the only one in the union that does it," Gibson answered. "But here is the best part. The state isn't that big and, according to Illinois law, all the witnesses must remain in the state."

Douglas jumped in and stole Gibson's thunder. "So some idiot in the Illinois state department has put all the witnesses in the same small town. Some small tourist town called Galena. Can you believe it?"

"That's messed up," Kidd agreed. "But I still don't see how this is a CIA issue."

"You're right," Gibson said. "It's an FBI problem. Or at least it should be." Gibson sighed.

"The FBI has a mole," Douglas said. "The Salvatore

syndicate has been tipped off that all of their rats are sitting fat and happy in Galena. Gibson believes that someone on his team leaked it."

"So the FBI has a mole." Kidd threw his hands up in the air. "Welcome to the club. The Salvatores have penetrated every level of government in almost every country on the planet. It's unbelievable." Kidd laughed and then continued, "But so what? They'll send some guys to kill all of these turncoats and everyone wins. Problem solved, right?"

"You're right," Gibson agreed. "That's exactly what they've done. The bodies have already started to appear. Apparently the Salvatore syndicate is so excited about wiping out these traitors, they're calling in their best assassin."

Recognizing the opportunity, Kidd sat up in his chair.

"That's what I thought too," Douglas said.

"The Sicilian? They sent the Sicilian to Galena?"

Douglas nodded. "It is the perfect storm. The perfect opportunity to take out the world's top assassin."

"Man." Kidd stood up. "For the first time ever, we know where the Sicilian is? You've got to be kidding me." Kidd was giddy with excitement. It was like Christmas morning. He had spent six years tracking down Salvatore's top killers. And these weren't your average street-corner-gang thugs. These guys were pros. They lived in the shadows. They had rock-solid aliases. They were nearly impossible to find. They had families. They looked and acted like everyone else. They could be your butcher or accountant. But the Sicilian was different. He didn't live in the shadows— he *was* a shadow. There were days when Kidd wondered if he was even real. Maybe the Sicilian was just a rumor. No one knew for sure.

Twice Kidd was certain he was close to catching him. But he came up empty-handed both times. But now Kidd would have the upper hand. He knew where the Sicilian was. And once he got a hold of the forty ex-Salvatore scumbags who were now in the witness protection program, he would even know who the Sicilian was going to kill. It felt like a neatly wrapped present had just been handed to him until Kidd remembered that they were talking about a town on US soil. "It would be illegal. The CIA can't operate inside US borders," Kidd said reluctantly.

"Technically this is true," Douglas agreed.

"But," Gibson interjected, "from what little I know, it seems like your team is the only group on the planet that might have the knowledge and skills to find and kill this guy. This Sicilian, as you call him."

"And," Kidd added, "technically we don't exist. *I* don't exist. How can I break a law when I don't exist? I'm black ops!"

"Exactly," Douglas agreed.

"This is really a job for Anton, though," Kidd said. "I could go in there and kill this guy. Believe me, nothing would make me happier. But people would notice. I'm good at what I do, but I'm not subtle. That's Anton's skill set. And that's how the Sicilian kills. They are both masters at making even the most bizarre deaths look like accidents. Anton thinks like the Sicilian. I think he'd be your best bet for finding this guy and killing him without drawing attention."

"I couldn't agree more," Douglas said. "And that's why I sent Anton and his family to Galena two weeks ago."

"Well, there you go," Kidd said. "Problem solved."

"Turns out he's having a hard time finding the Sicilian," Douglas said. "And the witnesses keep showing up dead. If we don't find the Sicilian soon, he will have killed all forty witnesses and disappeared back into the shadows forever."

Kidd sat down. "What do you mean Anton can't find him? It's not that big of a town, right?"

"Right," Gibson agreed.

"And Anton has the list of witnesses, right? I mean, he knows who the Sicilian is going to kill?" Kidd asked.

Douglas looked concerned.

"Okay," Kidd said. "I'll go to Galena. I'll find and kill the Sicilian. But it ain't going to be quiet."

CHAPTER SEVENTEEN

I*just sat and stared at the screen. Not only was my* mom Carson Kidd, she was an assassin? A weapons expert? She had never even shot a gun, as far as I knew. And to top it off, I'd traveled with her all over the world while she'd killed bad guys! How do you handle information like that? I took a deep breath and handed Emma her computer.

"Thanks," I said.

"No problem. Let me know if you need it again. It's a long trip." She slipped the computer into her bag.

I pushed back in my seat and tried to stretch my legs. Buses and planes were brutal for someone my height.

"Have you ever done this before?" I asked. "Ridden the bus?"

"No. This is my first time. I hate the hour train ride from Westport to Yale to see Andrew. I'm not sure how I'm going to sit for over twenty hours."

"Is that how long our ride is?"

"Something like that," she said. "You'll have another three hours from Chicago to Galena."

"Great. Do you go see Andrew up at Yale a lot?" I asked.

"Not a lot. He's superbusy with school and directing," Emma said.

"Oh. Directing? Like a play?"

"A musical. He's part of Dramat at Yale."

I assumed by the way she said "Dramat" that I was supposed to know what Dramat was. And I was clearly supposed to be impressed. I wasn't. I'd met enough private school punks over the years to know what they were like. Heck, my dad had been one. I said nothing. But I must have made a face.

"Hey," she said defensively, seeing the look on my face. "Andrew's a good guy."

"What? I didn't say anything."

"You didn't have to. But Andrew's not like that. He also rows crew for Yale."

"I'm sure he does." I smiled. "Ivy league, rowing, drama— I'm sure he's a normal great guy."

"Seriously!" she exclaimed. Her face was red. I'd hit a nerve. "How about you, mister?" she said, trying to change the subject. "Anyone special in your life?" she asked.

"Nope."

"Come on. There's gotta be someone? Somewhere?"

"Nope," I said. "I literally have nobody anywhere." And I didn't. No good friends. No family. Nothing left.

"So what's Andrew's musical about?" I asked.

"It's *Annie*," Emma replied.

"*Annie*?" I repeated. "At Yale? Isn't that, like, a kids' musical?"

"I know, it sounds a little crazy. But Andrew's vision for *Annie* is amazing. Really."

"His *vision*—for *Annie*?"

"Yeah, he's very excited. It's hard to explain. He describes it as sort of *Annie* meets *Hamlet*."

I said nothing. There was a long silence before Emma said, "You said you lost both of your parents? That sounds rough."

"What's this? You're changing the topic," I said.

"I'm a reporter. I'm always curious to hear the story. And I'm tired of talking about me."

"I don't want to bum you out," I said. "My mom died about seven months ago, and my dad died a couple of days ago. It hasn't been a great year." I stared at the seat in front of me. I had never talked to anyone about my mom. Or her death. And, obviously, I hadn't had a chance to talk about my dad or grandpa. At least not with anyone but Douglas. I don't know what it was about Emma, but I wanted to tell her everything. I wanted to tell her how much it had hurt when my mom had died. And how much it had hurt when my dad had stayed away after the funeral.

"Oh, I'm so sorry, Furious."

"No, it's okay." I continued to stare at the seat in front of me. "I've just never really talked about it before."

She stood up. "Here," she said. "Scoot over. I'm gonna sit on your side."

I slid into the seat next to the window, and Emma sat down next to me. She smelled great.

"What happened to your mom?" she asked.

"Oh, man. I'm not really sure." I rubbed my face. "It's kind of a long story."

She put her hands in the air. "Well, we've got nothing but time."

"It's not that I don't want to talk about it. It's just—just different. My life is different."

"*Your* life is different?" she said. "I'm dating a much older guy that's putting little orphan Annie's death to music, and you think *your* life is different?"

I smiled. "Right. Your life *is* messed up."

"You don't know the half of it," she said.

"So tell me. What is *so* messed up in Emma's world?"

"No, no. You first. You tell me what happened to your mom, and I'll tell you all about the incredible, caring, nurturing world that Tom and Cindy created for their lovely little Emma. That is, before Tom went off to jail."

"I bet Tom and Cindy have got nothing on Robert and Terri," I said.

"Oh." She smiled. "We'll see. Tell me about Terri."

"I don't know. I don't want to scare you away."

She gestured around again. "Where am I gonna go?"

I sighed. "All right, so what do you want to know?"

"What was she like?" Emma asked.

"What was she like? She was like a bear trap. Quiet but strong."

"A bear trap?"

"You asked. I'm just telling you the truth," I said.

"I've never heard anyone call their mom a bear trap."

"Well, you never met my mom," I said, wondering if I'd really known her myself. "Don't get me wrong—she was kind. She was great." Man, I wished we hadn't started this conversation.

"Did you guys get along?"

"Yeah, for the most part. We traveled a lot. And that was kinda messed up. Different cities and countries every few weeks. But we got along all right."

"You said you were something like an army brat. Was your mom in the military?"

"No. She worked as a consultant for the government," I lied. "I guess I never really knew for sure what she did for them exactly."

"The moving sounds rough."

"It got old."

"So what did you do for school?"

"New schools. All the time."

"Wow, I don't think I could do that," Emma replied.

"Yeah, well, it's amazing what you can do when you don't have a choice," I said. "How's that Portland, Oregon, childhood looking now?" I asked.

"I didn't grow up in Portland," she said. "The town I was raised in wasn't anything like Portland. How did your dad die?"

"He was shot," I said. "Just like my mom. The only difference being my dad was shot onstage right in front of me in a crowded ballroom."

"Oh my god, your dad was Robert Jones!"

CHAPTER EIGHTEEN

*E*mma and I stayed up most of the night talking. She wasn't kidding—her life hadn't been easy. Her parents had gotten mixed up in a cult back in Oregon. Some rich guy had bought up an entire town and brainwashed everyone. Everyone, including Emma's parents. Her childhood was far from normal.

I told her all about my screwed-up gypsy life. Or at least the life I'd thought my mom and I had lived. I didn't tell her about my mom being a CIA assassin. Or about how my dad had stolen my mom's stories and claimed them as his own.

Time seemed to stand still as Emma and I talked about our lives. I had never met someone so kind, smart, and funny.

"Oh, no!" Emma's voice suddenly cut through the quiet hum of the bus.

"What?"

"Look." She pointed outside. "The sun is coming up. We've talked all night!"

"Yeah." I smiled. "That's all right."

"No, it's not." Emma looked worried now. "I need to function today. I need to be amazing."

"Are we being a little competitive?" I asked as playfully as possible.

"You have no idea," she said.

Emma said she needed to get at least a couple of hours of sleep before we reached Chicago. I was too worked up and nervous to sleep. I had no idea what was waiting for me in Galena, but whatever it was, it had gotten my entire family killed. Emma let me use her laptop as she took a nap. I searched for information about Galena and ended up at the *Galena Gazette*'s website. It was the same paper that had concluded my mom's death was just a result of her being in the wrong place at the wrong time. I expected to see stories about corn prices and 4-H competitions, but the front-page headline read: ANOTHER GHASTLY ACCIDENT FOR GALENA.

Their website featured a couple of stories about how Galena was experiencing a rash of bizarre, deadly accidents lately.

I clicked and read the main article.

By all accounts, Derrick Triviski was a good man. A quiet man. "He kept to himself, really," Sue Lechner, an Apple Orchard Drive resident, said last night. "You barely knew he was around, really. Until tonight."

According to his neighbors, Mr. Triviski moved to Galena about a year ago and immediately landed a job at Bloom's Ace Hardware.

"He was a good worker," Gus Bloom, owner of Bloom's Ace Hardware, said. "He did his job and kept to himself. Not much of a talker."

According to Sheriff Daniels, Apple Orchard area residences reported hearing what sounded like a bomb going off around eight o'clock Thursday night. That loud boom turned out to be the explosion of Mr. Triviski's water heater.

"Oh yeah, my windows shook," Lechner said. "I'd never heard anything like it. Kind of odd that such a quiet man would go out with such a ruckus. And a water heater, no less. It really makes you think."

"We don't have anything conclusive," Sheriff Daniels said, "but it certainly appears that Mr. Triviski was simply in the wrong place at the wrong time."

According to Bloom, it is not that uncommon for water heaters to explode. "Oh yeah, it happens. It happens all the time. I heard about a guy over in

Hazel Green who had one blow through the roof and land a half mile away. Of course, I've never known one to take a person with it. That's kind of new. I heard they found his body and the water heater on top of old man Freedly's barn. Can you believe that? That has to be a quarter of a mile."

But, as many locals are quick to point out, Galena has experienced more than its fair share of uncommon and unfortunate accidents in the last several months. There have been well over a dozen bizarre accidents resulting in fatalities. And as unfortunate and bizarre as Triviski's water-powered rocket ride might be, the entire Galena area is still talking about the almost unthinkable string of events that took the lives of the entire Yaeger family earlier this year in the Galena River Bait Shop's leech tank.

CHAPTER NINETEEN

Emma *got off the bus in Chicago. She wanted to* exchange phone numbers, but I told her I didn't have a phone. Which was true, but I'm not sure she believed me. She gave me her number and told me to call her and let her know what I thought of Galena. But I already knew what I thought of Galena. I hated it. It was the place my mom died. I didn't care how quaint it was, I was going to hate it.

I stared out the bus window for three long hours after leaving Chicago. Illinois was painfully flat until we got close to Galena. Then the landscape started to change. The bus was finally finding some hills, and I could see actual bluffs in the distance.

We descended down a long and winding stretch of highway just outside of Galena, and I could see why Emma liked it so much. Galena really was just about perfect. The town was built at the base of a large bluff. Old brick buildings and tall church steeples dotted the hillside. It was . . . quaint. If you didn't mind a town full of mob informants and hit men.

I could see the river. And then I could see two massive floodgates on the edge of town with large walls and hills leading up to them. The gates were open but were clearly put in place to protect the main street, and downtown Galena, from flooding when heavy rain ran down from the hills, causing the river to rise. *Maybe they should close them now*, I thought, *and just trap all the criminals inside this tiny, violent, quaint little town.*

There was a sea of red and blue lights flashing not far ahead of us now. The bus driver slammed on the brakes, and several people fell out of their seats. It looked like some sort of roadblock.

"Is everyone okay?" the bus driver asked before coming to a complete stop. I looked around and everyone appeared to be all right. I stood up to try to get a better view of the road, but there were too many cars in front of us to see what was going on.

"I'm sure they'll get us moving again in a minute," the bus driver said.

Time dragged to a stop as I stared out the window for what felt like several hours. Finally, there was a knock on the bus door and an Illinois State Trooper stepped aboard. He talked with the driver for a few minutes and then turned and faced the passengers.

"Good evening, folks. I apologize for the wait, but I'm afraid there's been an accident," the trooper said. "Now, I know you're all real anxious to get to your final destinations, but I'm going to need you to be patient for a while longer while we contain the situation."

Contain the situation? What did he have to contain? Maybe someone had smashed into a truckload of chickens? Or cows? It could be hours if it was cows.

The noise level rose as the trooper turned to leave. I ran down the aisle and caught up to him as he was about to step off the bus.

"Excuse me, sir."

"Look," the trooper said, turning around, "I understand your frustration, son. But I'm asking you to be patient. Please." He began to turn back toward the door when I reached out and grabbed his shoulder.

"Sir," I said again as I took another step forward. "Galena is my final destination." I pointed to the floodgates protecting Main Street. "Is it all right if I just get off and walk from here?"

The trooper started to speak when the bus driver interrupted.

"Now, you go sit down. I'm not gonna start trying to unload luggage on the side of no highway."

I looked back to the trooper. "I don't have any luggage." I motioned down to the book in my hand. "I've got everything right here."

The trooper looked down at my book and then out the front window. "It's okay with me. But stay on the side of the highway and keep walking. I don't need any gawkers."

I quickly pushed past him before the driver could argue. There was a line of cars in front of the bus blocking my view of the accident. I walked down the shoulder toward town. I was a hundred feet down the road and I still couldn't see an accident. No cars. No cows. No chickens. It looked like every police and fire truck from every nearby town had been called to the scene. I kept walking toward Main Street. I was walking past a road flare when I saw the first one.

They weren't on the road. Nothing but cop cars and fire trucks were on the road. These were off to the side. Three neat crimson bricks evenly spaced about ten feet apart.

"Hey! Hey!" An officer was running toward me. He was yelling, "You can't be here." He had panic in his eyes.

"What's going on?" I asked.

"Son, you can't be here! You can't see this!"

"I'm just going to town. That guy back there said it was okay to walk into town!" I was pointing toward the town when my eyes connected with someone's eye. Or some*thing*'s. The eye was nested in the first of the crimson-colored bricks.

"Oh my god!" I screamed. "Oh my god!"

The cop was still yelling, but I couldn't understand a word he was saying. My eyes were darting between the three bloodred hay bales on the side of the highway. As I looked more closely, I could see that all three red-soaked bales were speckled with bits of fingers, arms, hair, and bones. My legs gave out and I fell to the ground as the cop continued to yell.

I got to my feet and ran. I kept running until I reached Main Street. I could have run all day, but I knew it was pointless. The bales of hay would be stuck there in my brain forever. Every detail. Every piece of bone would sit in my messed-up head forever. Next to the million other snapshots of my messed-up life.

I slowed to a walk as I passed the floodgates. There was a group of older men gathered on the sidewalk talking about a farm accident. *Farm accident?*

I felt sick as the image replayed in my head. I tried to push it out. I tried to think about something pleasant. I tried to think about Emma, but the hay bales kept coming back.

CHAPTER TWENTY

*M*ain Street was exactly as Emma had described it. Dozens of old brick buildings lined the long, narrow street on the other side of the floodgates. It was like stepping a hundred years back in time. Except for the stores. The Main Street businesses were the kinds of ma-and-pa shops and restaurants you would expect to find in a tourist town. I set out to find another pay-as-you-go phone. It had been more than twenty hours since I'd downloaded the last *Double Crossed* excerpt, and the new one had to be posted by now.

I walked up the north side of Main Street and found three wine shops, jewelry stores, and several cheese shops—but no mobile phone stores. I started back down the south side of the street and came across the toy store and candy store Emma had mentioned. I was about halfway back toward the floodgates when I felt the blood drain from my head. I stared up at the awning and my eyes began to well with tears. It was the DeSoto Hotel, and it looked nothing like it had in the black-and-white photo. I looked at the sidewalk. I got down on one knee and examined it. Of course, there was no trace of blood from where my mom's body had been. The broken glass had been fixed and the bullet holes in the door had been patched. There was no trace of the violence that had taken my mom from me.

"Can I help you?"

I looked up. There was a man in a suit offering his hand.

"Are you okay, son?"

I wiped the tears from my eyes, took his hand, and he helped me to my feet.

"I guess my knee gave out," I lied, staring into his kind eyes. Were those the last eyes my mom saw? I hoped so. I hoped they were his kind eyes and not the eyes of her killer.

"Just wait until you get to my age. The knees are the first thing to go." He laughed. "Are you going to be okay?"

"I hope so," I said. "I honestly hope so."

I continued walking down Main Street thinking about my mom. And my dad. And Grandpa. I decided, one way or another, I was not leaving Galena until the people that had wiped out my family paid for their crimes. If I needed to, I swore I would devote the rest of my life to bringing down the Salvatore crime syndicate.

CHAPTER TWENTY-ONE

I *decided to forget about the phone for the time being* and find a place to stay. I hadn't slept in almost forty hours and needed to lie down, at least for a few minutes.

Emma had said that the cheap B&B was located at the top of a long narrow staircase that had been cut into the bluff. I found the stairs between Cannova's Pizzeria and Ostby's Antique Store. I figured I'd see if I could get a room, or even afford a room, at the B&B before it got dark. And maybe someone there would know where I could buy a phone.

The stairs were steep and worn. I climbed for what felt like twenty minutes before I stopped. Was I even halfway up? I had to be halfway up. I stood for several minutes trying to catch my breath. I pushed myself against the railing to make room for a small group of people walking down the stairs. They were talking about the farm accident. Apparently news traveled fast in small towns.

I reached the top of the bluff after another ten minutes and two more breaks. The view was spectacular. I could see all of Main Street and the park and the river that ran behind Main Street. I could see the fire trucks still out on the highway. They appeared to be hosing down what was left of the farm accident.

The street that ran along the top of the bluff had been aptly named High Street and was lined with mansions that had been converted into quaint, and some not so quaint, bed-and-breakfasts. And, apparently, the B&B owners had decided to engage in a game of one-upmanship when it came to funny names for their inns. As I walked down the street looking for Betty's, I walked past the Stop on Inn, the Step Back Inn, the Dew Drop Inn, the Liv Inn, and the Butt Inn.

I found Betty's at the end of the block. Betty's was in desperate need of paint and the porch looked like it might come crashing down at any moment, but I was glad to see that Betty had decided not to participate in the name game that had consumed the rest of the block. The sign out front read BETTY'S BLUFF INN. Simple and pun-less. Under the name, someone had recently painted the words AND TAROT CARD AND PALM READING. I guess Emma had forgotten to mention that part.

A bell rang as I pushed the front door open. Betty's living room had been converted into some sort of astrological supply shop.

"I'll be right there," a woman's voice called from upstairs.

"No hurry," I yelled back.

There was a table in the middle of the room that had been covered in a purple sheet. A large crystal ball sat in the middle of the table. The walls were lined with make-shift shelves that had been cobbled out of old plywood and bricks. I walked along the shelves. Betty was selling all kinds of strange books, jewelry, crystals, candles, herbs, and do-it-yourself acupuncture kits. I thought about leaving, but where else could I stay so cheaply? Even the Butt Inn looked like it was probably more expensive than Betty's.

"Welcome to Betty's Bluff Inn."

I turned around to see an elderly woman with big curly orange hair walking down the stairs. She was wearing some sort of bright-colored robe or dress.

She continued her welcome. "Where the rooms are great, and we're not bluffing."

Oh, ouch. I was wrong. Betty *had* tried to participate in the name game. She just wasn't very good at it.

"Hi," I said. "I get it now—Bluff Inn. Like bluffing."

"That's us. Or me, anyway. I'm Betty O'Malley," she said, extending her hand.

"I'm—" I paused. I couldn't give her my real name. Even Betty was sure to have a computer. If she entered my name anywhere in it, Douglas and the CIA might find it. And me.

"I'm happy to meet you, Betty," I said. I shook her hand.

"Thank you," she smiled. "What can I help you with? A tarot reading, perhaps? Sage amulets? Love potions?"

"No. I'm just here for a room. I saw the fall colors special on your website."

"A room?" Betty questioned. I wasn't sure if she was worried about my age, or if she was just shocked to have a guest.

My mom and I had stayed in hundreds of hotels, motels, and B&Bs over the years, and I knew what kinds of questions the employees asked when booking a room. And I knew she would ask me for an ID. Even if she believed I was older than I was, she would still need an ID. I had my US military dependent ID in my wallet. But that had my age on it. There was no way this was going to work.

"Yes! Yes! Yes! The colors special. Perfect. Do you want to get started right away?"

"Ah, yes. Please."

"Perfect. Follow me," she said as she took five steps toward what used to be the dining room. The walls were covered with posters of the human nervous system, astrological signs, and weird astrology charts.

"Please lie down." Betty motioned to a table in the middle of the dining room.

"Excuse me?"

"Make yourself comfortable," she said, motioning again to the table.

I don't know if it was her kind smile or the fact that I was exhausted from staying up all night with Emma, but I climbed onto the table and lay flat on my stomach.

"Oh, no. Please lie on your back," Betty insisted. "I need to see your face."

"I don't understand," I said as I slid nervously off the table back onto my feet.

"I need to see your face. It is a big part of your aura. The colors are usually brightest around the face." She made a circular motion with her hands in front of my face.

"Aura?"

"Yes, dear. I need you on your back to read the colors of your aura," Betty said. Both of us looked a little confused.

Aura colors? The fall colors special had to do with reading aura colors and nothing to do with leaf colors.

"Oh," I said. "I don't mean to be rude, but is there any way we can do this later? I've been on a bus all night and I'm exhausted." I paused and decided to lie. "And unfortunately, I left my wallet on the bus and don't have my driver's license. But I do have cash."

"Heavens!" she said as she clapped her hands. "You had me so worried. Your colors are awful dark. Awful dark. But if you're tired, and have had such an unfortunate trip, that would certainly throw them off. Yes, let's get you a room.

We can do the reading later. When you're brighter."

"Thanks," I said, sounding truly relieved.

Betty walked to a desk in the corner of the living room. "You'll be staying until Friday?" she asked.

"How did you know that?"

"It's what I do, dear," Betty replied.

Was she referring to her experience as an innkeeper, or as some sort of fortuneteller?

Betty reached into one of the desk drawers and pulled out a clipboard. "What's your birthday, hon?"

"January twenty-sixth," I blurted out without thinking. That was my dad's birthday. Why had I selected my dad's birthday?

Betty said, "That's strange. You don't seem like an Aquarius."

"Oh?" I replied. She was right. I wasn't an Aquarius.

"Yeah. Aquarians are masculine. Tough-guy types. Aquarius is an air sign. I would have pegged you for an Earth sign. Probably a Taurus."

Right again, I thought. My birthday is May seventeenth.

"All the same," Betty said, "I'm going to put you in the Second House."

"Second House?"

"Yes," Betty replied. "The Second House is the house of Taurus. I got a feeling it's what you need."

"Okay by me." I had no idea what she was talking about.

"Okay, sweetie. Follow me."

I followed Betty upstairs to a door that featured a large painted bull and a small brass plaque that read SECOND HOUSE.

"Here you go, sweetie," Betty said as she touched my shoulder.

"Do I need a key?" I asked.

"No. No need for keys here." She turned and walked back down the stairs.

CHAPTER TWENTY-TWO

All four walls in the Second House had been painted emerald green and featured astrology symbols and hieroglyphic-like signs. Someone had painted the words WE OWN OUR EMOTIONS above the door. The only furniture in the Second House was a black futon bed and a dresser with three drawers. The top of the dresser had been covered with sand, a few smooth rocks, and a miniature rake made out of tree bark. I hung out in the Second House long enough to be polite. But the room absolutely gave me the creeps, and I needed to go find a phone.

Betty told me there was a Piggly Wiggly grocery store on the edge of town. She said she didn't have a car and the Pig was only a thirty-minute walk for her. It seemed like the Pig was the best bet for buying a phone in Galena, so I headed out.

I took the bluff stairs down to Main Street and walked back to the highway. There were a few people still standing around the accident site, but traffic was flowing now and the hay bales had been removed. Just the same, I was glad to be walking north. I walked for a mile and came upon Galena Senior and Junior High School. Someone had spelled out GO PIRATES with plastic cups stuck through the holes in the chain-link fence surrounding the football field. *Pirates?* In the middle of the country? Someone had a sense of humor.

I found the Piggly Wiggly about a mile past the school. I picked out the cheapest phone, two seven-dollar T-shirts, and a bag of minidonuts for dinner. The bill came to $69.87. That left me with $234, and it was only Saturday. There were five more days until my dad's book came out. Five days until I could tell the world that my dad's new book was 100 percent true. That whatever happened in the book was actually happening in Galena. But there was no way I could stay in Galena for five more days on two hundred bucks. Not if I wanted to eat.

I walked back to Betty's and closed the door to the Second House. I plugged in my new phone, and it chirped to life. I pulled up my dad's website, entered the code, and read the next excerpt.

There were many aspects of Carson Kidd's job that he would agree were difficult. Interrogating corrupt foreign officials was difficult. Running while wearing night-vision goggles was difficult. In the CIA, even the paperwork was difficult.

Carson Kidd could compile a long list of difficulties that came with his job, but spotting a trained killer, that was not one of them. That was easy. The CIA had volumes on the subject. They had entire manuals on assassin behavior. They had elaborate profiles, models, and statistics. And these weren't your typical Harvard professor touchy-feely hunches about the relationship between bed-wetting and serial killers. No, these were tried and true facts collected by studying killers. By creating killers.

But Kidd didn't need any of those studies to identify the killer standing in front of him now. He knew this guy was a killer, because they had been trained together. Anton and Kidd had become killers together.

Kidd was about to cross the street and approach Anton when Anton suddenly stopped and knocked on the front door of Cannova's Pizzeria. An Italian-looking man with long black hair opened the door and had a brief conversation with Anton. And then they both disappeared into the restaurant.

Kidd stood and stared. Did Anton know the guy in the restaurant? Was this part of Anton's cover?

And then Kidd remembered his training and realized he was standing still in the middle of a public sidewalk. He was drawing attention to himself. Kidd started walking slowly down the sidewalk, trying to blend in. He wondered if he would blow Anton's cover if he tried to connect with him in public. But as he pushed open the door to Cannova's Pizzeria, he figured he would pretend to not know Anton until Anton made it clear it was okay to talk.

Kidd stood in the doorway and lowered his left hand. It brushed against his hip. It was a subconscious move. He did it every few minutes without realizing. He only noticed the move when the bump from his faithful sidearm, his SIG, was missing. But it was there now and Kidd subconsciously felt safe as he walked into the restaurant looking for his coworker.

The pizzeria was one small room with a dozen linen-covered tables and brick walls. It looked nice. It looked like the kind of place Kidd would have enjoyed. Like the kind of place that would know how to make good gnocchi. He loved good gnocchi.

Kidd took a few steps into the restaurant. The floor creaked. He paused.

"Hello," a woman said as she walked out of the kitchen. "We don't open until noon, but I can bend the rules a little." She smiled.

"Oh, excuse me," Kidd said. "I thought I saw people coming in."

"Nope, just the staff. But you're welcome to stay. Or grab an apron and help out." She smiled again.

"Ah, that's okay. I'll just stop back later," Kidd said, heading toward the door. He stopped and turned. "How's your gnocchi?"

"The best in town."

"Perfect. I'll be back for dinner."

"We fill up this time of year. I'd be happy to make you a reservation." She walked to the podium by the door.

"Thank you. I'm serious about my gnocchi," Kidd said. "I like to enjoy dinner without a lot of people around. What time does it quiet down around here?"

"Our latest reservation is nine o'clock," she said, "but we're usually dead after eight."

"Nine would be perfect, then," Kidd said, thinking it might give him a chance to quietly connect with Anton.

"For one?" she asked.

"Yes."

"You won't be disappointed. Our gnocchi is out of this world. We have a wonderful new chef. He's Sicilian!"

"Sicilian?" Kidd asked. "What a coincidence. I know a guy from Sicily."

"And your name?" she asked.

"Carter Kenney," Kidd lied. "My name is Carter Kenney."

"Ah, your name sounds a little Irish," she said.

"More than a little." Kidd laughed.

"We'll see you tonight." She smiled again and set down the pencil.

Carter Kenney was not an alias Kidd had ever used before, but he hadn't missed a beat when asked. It was an old CIA alliteration trick. When making up a false identity, use your actual initials. It makes the alias easier to remember. It was the same advice the FBI gave to families entering the witness protection program. Heidi Strauss becomes Helen Stassen. Over the years, Carson Kidd had gone by hundreds of names but, for the rest of this trip, he would now be Carter Kenney.

Kidd had no idea what alias Anton was using, but he knew his real name. His name was Amado Anton. Kidd knew just about everything there was to know about Anton. He knew Anton was born in the Philippines and moved to the Hampton Roads area of Virginia when he was twelve. Kidd knew that Anton had joined the navy when he was eighteen and was quickly recruited into the navy's most elite fighting force, known as SEAL Team Six. He knew they both had been trained at The Farm. And as recently as two weeks ago, they were both members of the CIA. But what he didn't know was what Anton was doing here and who Anton had been talking to. Was the guy with the long hair the new Sicilian chef? Was he *the* Sicilian? Had Anton actually managed to find and get close to the Sicilian? If so, why hadn't he killed him yet? The kitchen at an Italian restaurant should have offered many opportunities to kill him. If, indeed, the man was the Sicilian.

CHAPTER TWENTY-THREE

I *lay on the bed thinking about my mom having to* come to this town to confront a killer. According to my dad's book, a world-class killer. The best killer. I'd always known she was tough. But I'd had no idea how tough she truly was.

I wondered if the Sicilian killed my mom. I wanted to skip to the end of the novel and see what happened to her. But according to my dad's book, Anton and the Sicilian both specialized in making assassinations look like accidents. I assumed that Anton, like my mom, was killed here in Galena. And I assumed that accidents like hot water heaters killing people and hay balers chewing people up and spitting them out hinted at the fact that the Sicilian was still here and still working his way down the list of witness protection rats.

CHAPTER TWENTY-FOUR

I *woke up feeling better than I had in a long time.* Maybe it was the magical effects of the Second House. Or maybe it was the fact that I hadn't slept on a bus. I glanced out the window. It looked perfect outside. I reached down to open the window when I noticed white sand, or salt, piled an inch high on the windowsill. I left it alone. Maybe there was something to Betty's crazy voodoo. I did feel great, after all.

I checked my dad's website, and there were two new excerpts available. I was starving and figured I'd read the first one over breakfast.

I found a copy of the *Galena Gazette* outside my door. I picked it up and walked downstairs. Betty was sitting at the small round table in the middle of the living room. The crystal ball was gone, and the table was now covered with tarot cards.

"Good morning, dear," Betty said, appearing to be deep in thought.

"Good morning."

"Say, honey, in all the excitement yesterday, I forgot to ask your name."

"I, ah—" I quickly tried to think of a name. I remembered Carson Kidd's advice about keeping your actual initials when making up an alias and, before I could stop myself, I blurted out "Finbar Jennings."

"Finbar? Well, that's an unusual name," Betty said.

"Yes, it is," I agreed.

I finally got a chance to try living with a different name and I came up with Finbar? Not Fred or Frank, but Finbar? I had gone to school with a Finbar for a while when my mom and I were in Ireland. For whatever reason, his name just came out. Stupid brain.

"Well, it is a lovely name. And, oh, you look so much brighter today. I told you, the House of Taurus was what you needed."

"The room was great, thank you," I said. I was just about out the door when I heard Betty call my name. Well, actually, Finbar's name.

"Yeah?" I responded.

"I know it is none of my business, but is everything all right?" Betty asked.

"Yeah. The room was perfect."

"No, I mean with you. Sometimes these cards are wrong, but . . ." Betty's voice trailed off as she looked back down at the tarot cards.

"Never better," I lied. "I'll see you in a bit." I quickly closed the door behind me on the off chance that my aura changed colors when I lied.

It was a perfect day outside. Not a cloud in the sky. I walked down High Street and took the stairs to Main Street. It was 8:30 a.m. and Main Street was already crowded with tourists. I grabbed a booth at a little diner and ordered eggs and a Coke.

I unfolded the *Gazette*. There was a small photo of Senator White and Attorney General Como along with a story about a recent presidential debate. According to the headline, Como had bested White and was one step closer to becoming the next president of the United States. But most of the *Galena Gazette* was devoted to the farm accident. There was a large color photo of the victims, Carl and Lily Freiburger. Apparently the Freiburgers had been new residents of Galena. And the story was quick to point out they were new to farming as well. Somehow they both wound up in the farm's hay baler. But no one was quite sure how. Although everyone interviewed agreed that hay balers were among the most dangerous pieces of equipment on a farm, and several farmers in the area had lost a finger or, in Joe

McDermott's case, an entire arm to a baler, no one had ever heard of a baler taking two whole bodies. Of course, no one, including me, had ever met the Sicilian.

The story went on to remind farmers to use extra care when baling this fall and listed some online resources for additional baling safety instructions.

I set the paper down as the waitress brought over my eggs. I wished I hadn't seen the picture of the Freiburgers. Looking at Lily's picture, I knew I had seen her eyes, or eye, before. I pushed my food away. I hated the way my photographic mind worked. All I could see now was Lily's eye resting in the bloodred hay.

The shrinks had called it eidetic memory. And it was just one more term in a long list of terms that had been assigned to me over the years. An army doctor in Germany thought it was tied to my ADHD. He said that eidetic memory went hand in hand with autism, too. He was darn near giddy when he told me. Like he had discovered something really cool and the connection would excite me, too. It didn't. I hated the fact that I had very little control over my mind. I didn't want to remember every single thing I had ever seen. Who would? The shrink may have called it eidetic memory, but I mostly called it a curse.

But for now, Lily's eye would not leave. I pushed the eggs around the plate, but I couldn't eat. I decided to walk down to the river and get some fresh air. Maybe I could find a place to sit and read the latest Carson Kidd excerpt on my phone.

CHAPTER TWENTY-FIVE

I *found a bench near Grant Park, next to the river.* Ulysses S. Grant had lived in this small town for, like, ten minutes when he was a boy, and they were trying to claim him as their own. Whatever it takes to pull in the tourist dollars, I guess.

I pulled out my phone and started reading.

> Carson Kidd went back to the DeSoto House Hotel and forced himself to sleep. It was a trick he'd learned over the years. You take sleep whenever, and wherever, you can get it. In his line of work, you never knew when the opportunity would arise again. He set the alarm for 8:45 p.m. and closed his eyes.

The alarm woke him several hours later. But it wasn't the alarm on the nightstand. This alarm was much louder. It was a fire alarm. Kidd got up and went to the window. It was dark now. There were a couple of tourists still down on Main Street. They were staring up at the DeSoto.

Carson moved to the door and his hand subconsciously brushed his hip. Once again he didn't notice the move, because his SIG was there.

Kidd took the stairs one flight down to the lobby.

"What's going on?" he asked one of the employees who was directing hotel guests toward the front door.

"Oh, I'm sure it is just some kid pulling a prank. I apologize for the inconvenience. We should have this straightened out in a few minutes. Please, feel free to visit Cannova's across the street and have a glass of wine on us," she said.

Kidd stepped out onto the sidewalk and looked across the street. Cannova's was packed with hotel guests. So much for the dinner reservation. And so much for quietly connecting with Anton. There were way too many people around. He decided he'd walk along the river. Maybe he'd stroll past Ulysses S. Grant's house and wait for the crowd to die down.

Kidd walked down a short side street that butted up to Grant Park. There was a long grassy knoll that ran to the edge of the river. The park was dark. Kidd started across the grass toward the river when he felt something tugging at his shirt. Before he could react, light exploded in his brain and he fell forward. He was facedown in the grass. His hand subconsciously went for his SIG, but it was gone. Then his hand reached for the back of his head. His hair was damp with blood.

"Slowly." A voice said in a heavy Italian accent. "Turn over slowly."

Kidd didn't recognize the voice. He had never heard the man speak, but he knew him the instant he laid eyes on him. It was the long-haired man from the pizzeria. It was the Sicilian.

"Well, well, well," Kidd said. "If it isn't the shadow himself."

"The shadow?" the man questioned. "I like that nickname."

Then the man repeated the name with his thick accent and lots of drama. "T-H-E S-H-A-D-O-W!"

"I like that!" He nodded his approval like a little boy. He was smiling now. "That is much better than the Sicilian."

The smile fell from his face.

"That, I don't like so much. It seems racist."

How did he know we called him the Sicilian? Kidd wondered. Had the mole in the FBI told him?

Kidd looked at the Sicilian's right hand. He was holding Kidd's trusty SIG.

The Sicilian noticed the glance and looked down at the gun.

"Oh, this?" the Sicilian questioned. "Don't worry about this." And with one smooth, swooping motion, the Sicilian threw the gun into the river.

"I don't care for guns. They're much too loud," the Sicilian said.

"Yeah," Kidd replied. "I've heard that about you."

The Sicilian watched Kidd stumble to his feet. Kidd was clearly still woozy from the blow to the back of the head.

"Now, this," the Sicilian said, pulling a giant knife from a sheath tucked in his waist. "This is the old-fashioned Sicilian way."

"I thought you preferred accidents," Kidd said, trying to buy time to formulate a plan. But his head wasn't working real well.

"Oh, I do, usually," the Sicilian answered. "But tonight I might just carve you up and dump you in the river."

"Aww," Kidd said, sounding disappointed. "Where is the creativity in that? Where is the artistry?"

The Sicilian started to walk around Kidd, sizing him up. "You're right," he agreed. "Maybe I'll dump a tackle box on you when I am done and make it look like you fell on your tackle box while fishing in the dark and you happened to get stabbed by your filleting knife."

Kidd was now circling with the Sicilian.

"Pretty weak, don't you think?" Kidd asked.

"Perhaps you are right. Perhaps I should ask my new friend Anton for a better idea. I've been very impressed with his creativity."

"What are you talking about?" Kidd tried his best to play dumb but disappointed even himself. "Who's Anton?"

"Please," the Sicilian dismissed. "I normally like to work alone, but I must admit to being impressed with your friend's skills. He is very good. A good addition to the team."

"Anton's working with you? Working for the Salvatores?" Kidd said. "I don't believe it." But, secretly, it confirmed Kidd's worst hunch. Kidd knew Anton was good. Too good to come to a small town like Galena with the list of people the Sicilian was sent to kill, and not be able to find the Sicilian. He never bought it. But he refused to believe his worst hunch.

"Fortunately, I don't care what you believe. I get paid to kill you, not convince you."

"Look, shadow," Kidd said mockingly, "I'll make you a deal."

The Sicilian laughed. "And what deal is this?"

Kidd said, "You drop the knife and take me to Anton or—"

The Sicilian laughed louder. "Or what?"

"Or else the locals are going to be picking up pieces of you in this park for the next couple of years."

"Anton told me about you," the Sicilian said. "He warned me that you were the toughest guy he had ever met. But I told Anton that I had met some pretty tough guys before. And none of them are still walking on this earth."

"Last chance, Sicilian. Take me to Anton," Kidd demanded.

"I told you that I don't like—"

Kidd spun around before the Sicilian could finish his sentence. They were nine feet apart. But Kidd moved fast. He closed the distance in an eighth of a second. The Sicilian had the knife in his left hand. And Kidd knew that many of the Salvatore assassins had been trained in several forms of martial arts and knife-fighting techniques. But so had Kidd. And Kidd knew that most martial arts training promoted balance and leverage. The Sicilian would go low. He was trained to go low. Another eighth of a second passed, and the Sicilian had already subconsciously started to widen his stance.

Kidd had been taught Krav Maga, a fighting technique, by an Israeli Special Forces trainer. Krav Maga was not about leverage and balance. It was about brutality and effectiveness.

Another eighth of a second passed. Kidd was now ten inches from the blade and closing fast. He made a motion as if he were about to tackle the Sicilian—a move the Sicilian would have expected. A move that Kidd knew would be suicide. No, Kidd decided, he would go high. He would just run up and over the Sicilian. He launched himself into the air and before the Sicilian could react, Kidd's right leg was over the Sicilian's left shoulder. And Kidd's left knee was smashing into the Sicilian's face.

Kidd's momentum knocked the Sicilian onto his back. Kidd landed three feet behind him in stride. He turned to see the Sicilian conscious but bloody. Kidd stepped on the Sicilian's left hand and kicked the knife hard with his right foot. The knife flew several feet and landed in the river. Then Kidd kicked the Sicilian in the head, snapping his neck. End of fight. End of the Sicilian.

CHAPTER TWENTY-SIX

Ilooked around the park. *I was sitting exactly where* Carson Kidd would have killed the Sicilian in my dad's story. Which meant, if all of *Double Crossed* was the true story of what happened to my mom here in Galena, I was standing exactly where my mom had killed the top Salvatore assassin.

I looked around the park. There were families playing, kids running, and couples holding hands. It all looked so normal. How many of these people were in the witness protection program? How many of them might be killers that had worked for the Salvatores before turning on them?

I was operating with the belief that my dad's book was 100 percent true. Which meant that my mom had killed the Salvatore assassin who had been sent here to kill the witnesses. But, judging from the recent accidents, the killing of the Salvatore turncoats had continued. Which meant that Anton was alive and well and still killing witnesses in Galena.

But Anton was also a CIA agent. And I would need proof that Anton had crossed over to the dark side if anyone was going to believe me. It seems like my dad had found the proof, but he was a highly trained and talented journalist. I had no idea what journalists did. I had no idea how to investigate. But I knew someone who did.

I took a piece of paper out of my wallet and dialed. Emma answered on the second ring.

"Hello."

"Yes, miss, we have come into possession of a garment bag that you might have accidentally left behind on your recent Greyhound trip," I said as seriously as I could.

"Ah, I don't think so. I mean—I have my bags."

"Well, this bag contained many strange articles."

"Strange articles?" Emma asked.

"Yes. Very strange. Including a very deranged—one might even say downright disturbing—script for a musical featuring a psychotic, murderous little orphan girl."

"Furious! I'm so glad you called!" Emma said.

"How is my favorite journalist?" I asked.

"Worried sick about you," she said.

"What do you mean?"

"Your grandpa's murder is national news, Furious. I mean front-page, on-the-television-twenty-four-hours-a-day news."

"Have they mentioned me?"

"Oh, yeah. They mention you every time they mention your dad."

"What are they saying?" I asked.

"They are saying you're dead, Furious. They are saying you died in the fire at your grandpa's house."

"What?" Douglas knew I was alive. He saw me hours after the fire. And the firemen wouldn't have found anyone in the house. "That doesn't make any sense."

"I know," Emma agreed. "Look, I'm no professional, but the journalist who broke that version of events must have been told in no uncertain terms that your body was in that fire. And it must have come from someone in authority, otherwise they would never report it."

"Right," I agreed. "You didn't tell anyone that you met me, did you?"

"No. I haven't told a soul that we met. But I think you need to call someone. You need to tell them you're all right."

Who would really care? I wondered. The only person that might possibly care was on the other end of the phone right now. And she knew I was okay. At least for now.

"I will. Soon," I replied.

"What is going on? Are you in danger?" Emma asked.

"I don't know. I'm hoping you can help me answer that."

"Me?" Emma's voice changed from concerned to scared. "How?"

"I need you to do a little research. I need you to look into a couple of people."

"Ah, Mister 'The Newspaper Is Gone. It's Dead.' now needs the skills of a trained journalist, huh?" Emma no longer sounded scared. Just overconfident.

"Yeah. Yeah. Help me out on this and I'll admit that it's a craft and that journalism will live forever. I'll yell it from the bluffs of Galena."

"Oh, how do you like Galena? Isn't it beautiful?"

"It is," I said.

"Did you find Betty's?"

"I did. You neglected to mention Betty's connection to the cosmos, though."

"Hey, I love Betty," Emma said. "Oh no, Furious, if Betty watches the news she'll see your name. It's not like you have a very common name."

"We're okay," I said. "I told her my name was Finbar."

"Finbar? Why Finbar?" Emma asked.

"Honestly, it was the first name that popped into my head. But what if they show pictures of me? She might recognize my face."

"No, because you're a minor, they couldn't run photos of you without your . . ." Emma's voice drifted.

"Parents' consent. Right," I said. "And I don't have parents or guardians or anyone."

"You have me," Emma said.

"Thanks. I appreciate it. So, can you do a little research for me?" I asked.

"Sure. Anything to hear you sing my praises. What do you need?"

"I'm hoping you can find out the name of the guy who killed my dad. I'm assuming they have released his identity," I said.

"He was killed at the scene, right?" Emma asked.

"Yeah," I answered as images of his face flooded my mind. "I'm trying to see if there is a connection between him and the Salvatore crime syndicate."

"The Salvatore crime syndicate? You're kidding, right? Tell me you're not mixed up with the Mafia, Furious." Emma sounded scared again.

"I'm hoping *you* can tell me if I am," I said. "I'm also hoping you can look into a death that might have happened here in Galena before my mom was killed. It would have happened near Grant Park, and the dead guy would have been Italian. Well, Sicilian, actually."

"Furious! Please! Just get on the bus and come back to Chicago. I'll help you get out of whatever mess you're in."

"Thanks, Emma," I said. "I really do appreciate your concern, but trust me, any information you can find will be a huge help to me."

There was a long silence.

"Emma?"

"Okay," she whispered into the phone. "I'll see what I can do."

"If anyone can do it—"

"Yeah, yeah," she said, cutting me off. "Is this your phone number?"

"Yes."

"I'll call you soon. Stay safe."

I hung up and thought about Douglas. Why would the authorities say I was dead? They had no body to prove it. Plus, Douglas knew I was alive. Was he running the cover-up? My dad's book said the Salvatores had penetrated every level of government. And my grandpa seemed to think Douglas was involved in my parents' murders. If he convinced the world I was already dead, then he'd be free to hunt me down and kill me. No one would be looking for a dead guy.

I spent the rest of the morning hiking the bluffs of Galena, trying to stay out of sight. I didn't need Anton spotting me. And who knew where Douglas was. I had ditched my phone in New York, but maybe the CIA could see my Web-browsing history. It would show my last search was looking for a bus to Galena.

CHAPTER TWENTY-SEVEN

I *got back to Betty's a little after three. Betty was wait-*ing for me in the living room.

"Well, Finbar, what do you think of our little town?" Betty asked as I closed the door behind me.

Why had I said my name was Finbar? Could I correct it now? Maybe I could say, *"Finbar"? Oh no, you must have misunderstood me. My name is Dave.*

"The town is good," I lied. It was a town full of mobsters and killers. One of which probably killed my mom. I hated the town.

"Isn't it? I just love this place. It's the galena in the ground that gives it the special vibe," Betty said.

That was an odd way to put it. "Yeah, the ground, or, ah, the bluffs are pretty cool," I said.

"No, I mean the mineral. Galena the town was named after galena the mineral. It's all around us here. And it gives off such a wonderful cleansing spirit."

"Oh, right. Cool," I said.

"Well, I'm all ready for you." Betty motioned to the table. "I've prepared something very special just for you."

The table was draped in bright neon-colored sheets. Just like the ones Betty was wearing.

"What's all involved with this?" I asked nervously as I motioned to the table.

"I'll align your spirits. Trust me, you'll feel great," Betty said.

I had to admit I had felt great when I woke up in the Second House. And it was hard not to trust Betty, so I sat down on the table. She had me take off my shoes and lay faceup on the table. She started clapping, rubbing, and waving her hands above me. She was repeating something. I wasn't sure what I should look at, so I just closed my eyes.

"Sweetie, you are so out of balance. The galena will be good for you this week. But you are out of sync. Oh wait, just a minute," Betty said as she walked into the other room and came back with a large pointed crystal on a leather rope. She hung the crystal directly over my forehead.

"Try not to move."

I laid still while she spun the crystal above me. She repeated the process over various parts of my body. She seemed extremely disappointed with the results.

"Oh, hon," she kept saying. "Oh, dear, dear, dear."

Betty started placing crystals on me. She placed one in the middle of my forehead. Over what she called my "third eye." And then she placed three crystals on my mouth.

"Do you know what a chakra is?" she asked.

"No," I muttered beneath the crystals.

"'Chakra' is derived from the Sanskrit word meaning 'round' or 'wheel.' Your chakra should be spinning effortlessly. It should be bright and brilliant."

"I take that to mean mine is dull and slow?" I asked.

"Oh, hon. You just need help. Someone to show you the way. Look at me."

I tried to turn and look at her.

"See how my energy flows?" Betty asked.

I saw nothing.

"These crystals will help your chakra flow. They will help balance you. You have so much negativity and anger for someone so young."

Right again, I thought.

Betty spent the next two hours piling rocks on me, lighting candles, burning herbs, and waving her hands. Call me crazy, but I actually felt better when it was over.

I sat up and Betty put a necklace around my neck. She

made me promise I wouldn't take it off. She said it was some sort of protective amulet. It looked like a giant blue eye. It actually reminded me of Lily Freiburger's eye. But who was I to argue with Betty? Clearly I needed protection, and I decided I would take it in any form I could get it. But I did decide it was best to wear it under my shirt.

CHAPTER TWENTY-EIGHT

When *I got back to my room, I found that Betty* had hung another giant eye above the futon in my room. It was painted on a sheet of plywood and hung from a rope. I grabbed the last of my Piggly Wiggly minidonuts and sat down on the futon. I pulled up my dad's website and downloaded the next excerpt from *Double Crossed*.

> Kidd loaded the Sicilian's body into a canoe from a nearby dock and paddled downstream. He dragged the canoe ashore about five hundred yards downriver. He searched through the Sicilian's clothing and found a wallet with over one thousand dollars in cash and an ID with a Galena PO box for an address. The

picture on the ID looked like the Sicilian's, but the name read James Dutton. Kidd stuck the cash and ID in his pocket and flipped the canoe over to conceal the Sicilian's body.

The crowd had died down by the time Kidd got back to Cannova's Pizzeria.

"Ah, Mr. Kenney," the hostess greeted Kidd. "I was starting to wonder if we would see you tonight."

"Yeah, I apologize for being late." Kidd motioned across the street to the DeSoto House Hotel. "I had some fires to put out."

"My hero." She smiled. "Well, I have a table ready for you."

Kidd ordered gnocchi and a glass of Zinfandel. And the hostess had been right: The gnocchi was out of this world. Maybe even the best he'd ever had.

"I'm so glad you liked it," the hostess said, clearing the empty dish from the table.

"Say, maybe you can help me out," Kidd said.

"Sure, what's up?"

"Well, I was supposed to meet a friend of mine here," Kidd lied. "Actually, he works here. But I haven't seen him all night."

"Who's your friend?" the hostess asked.

"James," Kidd said. "James Dutton."

"Yeah." She now looked a little surprised. "Well

we haven't seen him either. That's why I'm bussing." She motioned to the dishes in her hand. "He didn't show up for work tonight."

"Well, that's odd," Kidd said. "Does he work another job? He told me to meet him at work. But this was the only work he's ever mentioned."

"No. This is it. And it's very unlike James to just not show up. He's very prompt and very dependable."

"Right." Kidd nodded. "Do you happen to know where he lives? Maybe I'll check in on him."

"Yeah. He lives down the block, above Dirty Gert's bar."

"Dirty Gert's?" Kidd asked.

"Yeah, room 22B. Take the stairs up from the alley. You can't miss it."

"Great. Thanks again. The gnocchi was perfect."

Kidd paid the bill with the Sicilian's cash and stepped out onto Main Street. Most of the tourists were gone now, and Galena didn't appear to have much nightlife.

The alley behind Main Street played host to a labyrinth of old wooden staircases and planks that led to the apartments above the Main Street shops. Kidd found the Sicilian's apartment a couple of blocks down from Cannova's. The apartment was dark, and a white lace curtain blocked his view into it. Kidd tapped lightly on the glass and waited. He slid the Sicilian's fake ID between the door and jamb. The door popped open without any force.

Kidd stepped inside and his hand subconsciously went to his hip. No SIG. Kidd suddenly remembered his SIG was at the bottom of the Galena River. He closed the door behind him and wished he had fished the gun out of the river. Maybe he still would.

Kidd stood still as his eyes adjusted to the dark. It appeared to be a one-room place. He could make out an unmade bed in the middle of the room and a countertop that served as the kitchen. He carefully walked to the counter and searched the drawers for a knife. He found a butter knife. It would have to do.

He turned on a lamp. The place was a dump. There were food wrappers and empty beer bottles everywhere. Kidd searched the entire apartment, but found nothing. No clues as to who the Sicilian was or who he would kill next. And no indication that anyone else was living here. Kidd knew that Anton had been sent into Galena with his daughter and would most likely be staying in nicer conditions. Douglas often liked to have his agents travel with their families. He felt reality was the best cover. Who would suspect a parent traveling with kids would ever be a CIA assassin?

Other than a couple of shirts in the dresser, a toothbrush in the bathroom, and trash on the floor—there was no real sign that anyone lived here. There wasn't anything in the refrigerator. There weren't any papers, books, money, glasses, or weapons—nothing.

Kidd shoved the butter knife into his pocket and turned off the light. He moved a vacuum, bent down, and peered out the window into the alley. He stared out the window for several minutes, watching for movement. Nothing. No one was out there. He stood up to leave and glanced back down at the vacuum. Then Kidd flipped the light back on. The vacuum bag appeared full. Kidd looked around the room. The floor was covered with trash. How could the vacuum be full? Clearly the Sicilian hadn't vacuumed. Clearly he didn't care about cleanliness. He hadn't even attempted to throw anything away. Kidd bent down and unzipped the vacuum bag, and a photo album fell out of the bag onto the floor. Kidd thumbed through the photo album. Page after page was the same thing. Every page had a photo on the left and then either an obituary or some newspaper clipping detailing some horrible death on the right. Kidd immediately knew what this was. Although not as crude, Kidd had created similar books for the

CIA. Professional killers called them proof books. They were photo albums identifying targets. The targets were to be killed, and it was the assassin's job to provide proof of the kill. Proof could be a picture of the murder scene, a copy of the police report, an obituary . . . anything that established the target was dead.

Kidd was sickened as he flipped through the photo album. Normally, a hit would consist of one or two people. Maybe a family, if the circumstances absolutely called for it. But this book was huge, and the Sicilian had already killed over a dozen people. In fact, Kidd was only able to find two photos that did not yet have a proof of death. One was of a woman who looked to be in her forties and, on the last page of the book, he found the photo of a young girl. She was maybe sixteen years old and had long dark hair and green eyes. She was beautiful, but she looked tough. Like maybe she had seen things a young girl shouldn't see. But she was alive. Or at least there was no obituary next to her photo—yet. As Kidd shoved her photo in his pocket, he made a promise to himself that it would stay that way.

•••

Kidd decided to go for a run the next morning before heading over to talk to the local sheriff. He wasn't sure how the sheriff would react to Kidd killing someone in the sheriff's town. Even if that someone was a killer for hire. And Kidd wanted to run because he wasn't sure when he would be able to stretch his legs again.

And what a run it was! The sheriff and residents of Galena had obviously taken great care to create the perfect example of small-town middle America. Most of the houses lining Grant Park had a porch and an American flag out front. Like it was mandatory. Main Street itself was so clean you could practically eat off of it. And Kidd wasn't surprised to see the flower boxes below the barred windows on the Main Street jailhouse. Nor was he surprised, during his postrun visit to the sheriff's, to find out that the man was less than excited to hear about any problems arriving in his perfect little town.

"Whoa, boy. Let's start again," Sheriff Daniels said.

"You're going to get a report of a stolen canoe," Kidd said.

"Yeah?"

"I stole the canoe," Kidd said. "Well, really I borrowed it."

"Yeah?" The sheriff's head was now slightly cocked to the side.

"You'll find the canoe about five hundred yards downriver from town."

"Why are you telling me this?" Sheriff Daniels asked.

"'Cause you're going to find the body of James Dutton under the canoe."

"And how do you know this?" the sheriff asked.

"I put him there. I killed him."

The sheriff stood up now. "You don't say."

"But his name isn't James Dutton."

"It isn't?" Sheriff Daniels questioned. "Then what is his name?"

"I don't know," Kidd said. "I'm with the CIA, and we've been trying to get this guy for years. We just called him the Sicilian."

"The Sicilian?"

"Yup," Kidd replied flatly.

"And what did you say your name was?" the sheriff asked.

"It's Kidd. Carson Kidd. Look, I know you'll need time on this. And I know you'll need to check me out, but I've got a question first." Kidd paused as he pulled the photo of the girl out of his pocket.

"You've got a question?" the sheriff said in a mocking voice.

"Do you recognize this girl?"

But the sheriff didn't need to answer. Kidd could tell by his reaction that he knew her.

"What can you tell me about her?" Kidd asked.

"Tell you? Tell you?" The sheriff chuckled, but Kidd could sense his unease. "I can tell you nothing. Now, let's start this thing again. Do you have some sort of ID?"

•••

Kidd had seen the inside of many jail cells, but he was positive that Galena's was far and away the nicest. He spent six hours in the cell while Sheriff Daniels checked out his story. Even the cell bunk beds were comfortable.

It was dinnertime before the sheriff came to let him out.

"Look, I'm not happy about this," Sheriff Daniels said. "I'm letting you go for now, but you're done with your CIA stuff in my town, got it?"

"Who's the girl?" Kidd asked, ignoring the sheriff's demands.

"Didn't you hear me? You've got no jurisdiction here. You're out of the game. Your boss, Douglas, wants you back at Langley. And I want you out of Galena."

"The girl's in real danger," Kidd said.

"I don't see how. We fished the Italian Dutton

guy out of the woods. Thanks to your handiwork, he ain't gonna be hurting anyone."

"Trust me. She's in trouble."

"Trust you? That's a laugh. You won't even tell me what you're investigating in my own town."

"I told you, I'm on vacation."

"Vacation? Right." The sheriff chuckled again.

"I know how it looks, but it's true," Kidd lied.

"Well, since you're into telling the truth, why don't you tell me what kind of danger the girl is in?"

"Serious danger," Kidd answered.

"Uh-huh. That's what I thought. It's all one direction with you CIA guys. You want me to tell you everything, while you tell me nothing." The sheriff started walking away.

"There's another guy. There is a dangerous guy in town named Anton and, sooner or later, he's going to kill that girl," Kidd said.

"And I don't suppose you can tell me how you know that?" the sheriff asked.

"No."

"That's what I figured," the sheriff sighed. "Do you have a photo of this Anton?"

"Trust me, there are no photos of Anton. And he will not be using his real name."

"So, let's say for a minute that you're right," the sheriff said.

"I am right," Kidd replied.

"Well, let's say you are. How do I help this girl?" the sheriff asked.

"Let me help you," Kidd said. "Who is she?"

"I can't tell you," the sheriff said.

"Then I can't help you."

"I'd be breaking a dozen different laws if I told you," the sheriff answered.

"Because she's in the witness protection program? Trust me, that's not a secret," Kidd said. "To anyone."

Kidd pulled a picture of the woman from his pocket. "I'm guessing she's in it too."

"How did you know?"

"You have to take me to them," Kidd said. "We have to move them now."

CHAPTER TWENTY-NINE

I *stared up at the ceiling. I thought about my mom.* How accurately had my dad documented my mom's experience in Galena? Was it 100 percent factual? If the story was an exact account of what had happened, then the Sicilian, or James Dutton, would have to have lived in apartment 22B above Dirty Gert's. Before my mom killed him, that is. I knew Dirty Gert's was real enough because I saw it on Main Street. I decided to walk over to the Piggly Wiggly to pick up dinner, and then maybe I'd go knock on the door of 22B and see if a guy named James used to live there. It seemed like as good a plan as any.

I'd just reached the highway when my phone rang.

"Hello."

"Hey, Furious, it's Emma."

"My favorite reporter," I said. "Did you have any luck?"

"Sort of." Emma's voice sounded shaky. "I'm more convinced than ever that you need to go to the police and ask for help. The guy who killed your dad was a really bad dude, Furious."

"I kind of figured that part out myself," I said. "Shooting my dad was my big clue."

"Ha-ha. His name was Anthony Gruber. He's been in and out of trouble most of his life. Aggravated assaults. Grand larceny. Racketeering. That kind of stuff."

"Sounds like mob stuff," I said.

"It is."

"What are larceny and racketeering, anyway?" I asked.

"Theft, gambling, that kind of stuff. Gruber definitely had ties to the mob. And most of the stories said he was associated with the Salvatore crime syndicate."

Emma paused and I said nothing.

"Why would the mob want to kill your dad, Furious?" Emma asked.

"I think it has something to do with Galena and my mom's death. Did you get a chance to look into the guy who was killed in Galena? Possibly a Sicilian or Italian guy?"

"No, not yet. I've got to run to this group dinner, and then I'll look into after."

"I appreciate it," I said. "I'm running to dinner too. Give me a call later."

"Oh, where are you going to dinner?" Emma asked. "Because there is an awesome little Italian place called Cannova's on Main Street."

"So I hear," I said. "No, I think the Piggly Wiggly is more in my budget."

We said good-bye, and I ran the rest of the way to the Pig.

I threw two Cokes and a box of Famous Amos cookies on the conveyor belt and waited more than ten minutes for the woman in front of me to finish checking out. She was talking to the checkout girl about something that seemed to make them both quite upset. I figured it was about the Freiburgers and the hay baler accident, but who knew in this town. It could have been any number of bizarre deaths. Hot water heaters. Leeches. And whatever else Anton could cook up.

I looked over the products for sale next to the register. Small towns sure were different. Back east, you would normally find gum, candy bars, and batteries at checkouts. But the Pig was selling hunting knives, horse accessories, and sheep shears.

The girl behind the counter wore a red shirt with a name tag that said HI MY NAME IS TRISH. And she wore a long black tie dotted with a cartoon pig. The pig looked like a rip-off of Porky Pig.

"I hope that's not dinner," the girl said, pointing to the cookies.

"It is," I said. "But I'll have you know that Amos was

famous because he lived to be one hundred and five—eating mostly these cookies."

"Really?" she asked.

"Really," I lied. I had no idea if there was even an Amos. But Trish had a great smile.

"Were you friends with the Freiburgers?" I asked.

"The whats?"

"The Freiburgers. The couple in the accident. I thought I overheard you talking about the baling accident."

"Oh god," Trish covered her mouth. "I didn't know it was *two* people that went through the baler! God, that must have been a mess."

"It was," I said.

"No, Mrs. Lucas and I were talking about Mr. Schneider. He's the—" She paused. "He *was* the gym teacher at school. They found him dead in the gym." Trish lowered her voice. "He was hanging from that damn rope he made us climb. A group of cheerleaders found him. I guess it was some sort of freak accident."

"Oh. Wow." I had no idea how to respond to that. Did these people really think one town could see this many freak accidents?

"I'm glad," Trish said. "Not that Mr. Schneider is dead. But I'm glad that those witches had to find him like that." Trish paused and looked at me. "Oh crap, I've never seen you before—you're not Schneider's nephew or something?"

"Aahhhh," I said, speechless. What do you say to a girl who's glad the cheerleaders found a dead guy?

"You're not from around here, are you?" she asked.

"No," I said. "I'm not."

"Oh, god. Now I sound awful. You have to know those girls to understand the depth of my justifiable hatred."

"Okay," I said. "I believe you."

CHAPTER THIRTY

It took me twenty minutes to walk back to Main Street. I sat down on a bench and ate my dinner. I was just about to eat the last cookie when my phone rang. It was Emma.

"Hey, that was pretty quick," I said.

"Yeah, dinner was kind of boring, so I bailed."

The image of Lily Freiburger's eye staring at me from the hay bale popped into my mind as Emma said "bailed." I hated the way my mind worked. I put the last cookie back in the box.

"It didn't take me long to verify that there was an Italian national who died a couple of months ago in Galena."

"Really?" I asked. "Do you know what his name was?"

"James Dutton," Emma said.

James Dutton was the Sicilian's alias. Obviously the Galena police never figured out James's real identity.

"Yeah," Emma continued. "Apparently he died trying to steal a canoe."

"That must have been some canoe," I said.

"Yeah, they said he slipped and broke his neck. They actually found him under the canoe."

"Oh, yeah?"

"You don't sound convinced," Emma said.

"I'm not."

"You don't think it was an accident?"

"I know it wasn't," I said.

"Care to tell me how you know?"

Emma sounded like a reporter now.

"Tell me more about this trip you're on," I said.

"You're trying to change the topic," Emma said.

"No," I said. "I'm serious. You said it was for young journalists, right?"

"Yes. The top high school writers from around the country were invited to spend ten days at Northwestern and work on the craft. One of us will even get to write a feature story for the *Chicago Tribune* before we leave. Why?" she asked.

"I might have the story of a lifetime for you," I replied honestly.

I told Emma that she would have the first crack at the

largest story of the year, but I needed a couple more days to put the pieces together and find some proof.

"Proof of what?" she asked.

"You'll see. I'll call you soon."

I slipped my phone into my pocket and headed to Main Street. To apartment 22B.

CHAPTER THIRTY-ONE

Main Street was deserted when I got there. And Dirty Gert's was closed for the night. I walked around the block and down the alley that ran behind Gert's. The alley was a mess of rickety old stairs and catwalks. It looked more like parts of Thailand than Illinois.

The staircase shook as I climbed to the second level and stood outside 22B. What now? God, this was a bad idea. There was a curtain over the door's window. The apartment looked dark, but the reflection from the alley light made it difficult to know for sure. I cupped my hands over my face and pressed against the glass when—

BEEP BEEP!

BEEP BEEP!

BEEP BEEP!

My heart raced. I was shaking. My pocket was shaking. It was my phone. I reached into my pocket just as a light came on inside the apartment.

Crap! Should I run? Hide?

The door swung open. "Who's there?" A woman stepped out onto the catwalk. "Who are you?"

"Ah, I'm looking for James?" Man, what if she was with the Salvatores too?

"There's no James here," she said.

I tried to look over the woman's head into the apartment. It looked just like my dad had described it in the book. Or, perhaps more actually, like my mom had described it to my dad.

"I said there's no one by that name here." The woman rose up on her toes in an effort to block my view.

"Do you know where he went?" I asked.

"If he's the guy that lived here before me, I think he's dead," she said as she stepped back into the apartment and closed the door.

I made my way up the bluff stairs, thinking about the Sicilian. My dad had written that he was the best assassin in the world. And Anton was one of the CIA's best killers. Now he had turned out to be a traitor and was working for the Salvatores. So Galena was full of ex-Mafia bad guys turned rats and one highly talented CIA assassin sent here to kill them all. Or, at least all the ones that the Sicilian had not already killed.

I knew I would find out soon enough who killed my mom. The whole world would find out on Thursday when my dad's book came out. My mom's killer would be Carson Kidd's killer in the book. And based on the title *Double Crossed,* my money was on Anton.

But thanks to the popularity of my dad's books, almost everyone on the planet would read the book. And with my dad using all real names this time, it wouldn't take people long to realize the book was a true story. And with his name and the names of his victims in print, it wouldn't take Anton long to go into hiding. Even though Anton's name was in the excerpts, I doubted he was a big fan or avid reader.

I twisted the handle to Betty's Bluff Inn and pushed the door open. The living room was dark and I hurried up to the Second House. I sat on the futon, under the giant eye, and thought about my dad's story. I needed to find Anton before the book came out on Thursday. Before he could slip into the shadows. I wanted revenge. I wanted justice. But I would need proof. Who would believe a twelve-year-old kid? Especially a kid who, according to the media, wasn't even alive.

I thought about the Sicilian's apartment. And the photo album he used to record his hits. If I could get ahold of the photo albums with the names of the people killed, and those names matched up with actual dead people—that would be enough proof. Then Emma could write a story about how my dad chronicled my mom's death and the murders of dozens and dozens of witnesses in Galena. That would do it. The world would have to pay attention.

But how could I do that? The Sicilian was dead and Anton was trained to not be found. By anyone! Certainly not a twelve-year-old kid. I had no idea what he even looked like—or did I? Maybe my messed-up photographic memory would come in handy. According to my dad's book, my mom and Anton had trained together at the CIA's assassin training grounds. So maybe they had worked together too. Maybe Anton had been in the same cities as my mom and me. My mind would register a faint flicker of recognition if I had ever seen Anton. Even if I don't realize it. If he ever stood in line with us at an airport or coffee shop, pretending not to know my mom, there was still a chance I would feel something. Some deep, distant tingle in the back of my mind that would tell me this person was familiar. I made a mental note to pay attention to those faint feelings this week.

I thought about Anton again. My dad had said he was the best. That he got the important jobs. The *can't miss* hits. And, according to my dad's book, he worked fast. In fact, there were only two people left on his list when Carson Kidd killed him. My dad had written that there was a woman in her forties and a young girl. He wrote that the girl in the photo was about sixteen years old with long dark hair and green eyes. The book said she was beautiful but tough. It also said she was alive. Maybe that was still true. Everything else in my dad's book had proven true so far. And my mom had killed the Sicilian before he could finish his job. If I couldn't find Anton, maybe I could find one of the targets. Alive. And Emma could write the story of the girl who survived. The girl whose name will be in my dad's book when it comes out on Thursday. Maybe that would be enough to get people interested. It was a long shot, but it was all I had.

It wasn't all that crazy. She would be a lot easier to find than a CIA-trained killer. The book said she was sixteen. Which meant there was only one place she could be tomorrow morning: Galena High School—assuming my mom hadn't moved her before she was killed. The school was on the way to the Pig. There was a chance that the proof I needed might be a sophomore or junior at Galena High School tomorrow. I knew she had long dark hair and green eyes. I knew it was a long shot, but it was the only shot I had. I set the alarm for 6:15 a.m. and decided to go try to find out.

CHAPTER THIRTY-TWO

I *woke up before the alarm went off. It was 6:15 a.m. I* had no idea what time school started, but I figured I should get there early. No one was around at Betty's and I quietly slipped out the door and set off for Galena High.

I wasn't worried about showing up at a school I didn't go to. I had spent most of my academic career bouncing from one school to another. I knew it would take days, maybe even weeks, before the school would realize my paperwork and transcripts weren't ever going to arrive. And I'd be long gone by then. There was no point in me staying in Galena after my dad's book was released. Anton's name and actions would be known worldwide and he'd disappear. And I wasn't too worried about passing as a high school student.

At my height, everyone always assumed I was older.

I stopped at the Pig on the way to school and bought a Mountain Dew, a few cupcakes, a five-subject notebook, and a pen. The total was $12.67.

I sat down on a small hill next to the school, ate my breakfast, and watched the parking lot start to fill up. A woman in a pink suit was standing in front giving an interview to a reporter. I assumed she was the principal.

As I walked past her, I heard her say something about Schneider and the cheerleaders. She had a dead teacher to deal with. It was going to be a long week for her. She was going to have a lot more to worry about than who I was and why my paperwork was missing.

Galena High was nice. Much nicer than most of the cinder block military base schools I had attended. It actually looked a lot like my New Canaan school, except the Galena students weren't showing up in Ferraris and Porsches.

I wandered around for a few minutes before finding the office in the basement. There was a large group of teachers standing behind the counter. They stopped laughing as I walked in. I guess I wasn't going to be privy to the teacher jokes.

"Can I help you?" an older woman asked, stepping away from the group and approaching the counter.

"Yes, I'm—" Oh, geez. I hadn't thought about a name. I couldn't use Furious. Furious was supposed to be dead. Should I just use Finbar? I hated it more than Furious, but

I wasn't coming up with any other good *F* names in the moment.

"I'm Finbar. Finbar Jennings."

"Yes?" She looked puzzled.

"I'm a new student. It's my first day," I said.

"A new student?" she repeated.

"Yes, ma'am."

She turned toward the group of teachers. They were laughing again.

"Carol, do you know anything about a new student? I didn't see anything on the report."

Another woman stepped to the counter.

"What new student?" Carol asked.

"He says it's his first day."

Carol looked at me. "Are your parents with you?"

"My mom is still overseas. I'm staying with my aunt. I'm transferring from an international school in Italy. I bet they're just slow on sending paperwork."

"Italy? Wow. A world traveler," Carol said.

The door slammed behind me. I turned around to see the woman in the pink suit. She didn't look happy. The group dispersed quickly.

"Ah." Carol looked at the woman in pink and then back at me. "We'll get this straightened out. What grade are you in, hon?"

"Tenth," I lied.

She was now filling in some sort of form on the computer. "Can you spell your name for me, please?"

I spelled Finbar's name and gave her the name and address of a school I had attended in Italy.

"And you said you're staying with your aunt here in Galena?"

"Yes."

"And who is your aunt?"

Galena was a very small town. I was sure Carol knew everyone. She would know if I was lying. I decided to go with the only person I knew in Galena.

"Betty O'Malley," I said.

"Betty O'Malley? From Betty's Bluff Inn?" Carol asked.

"Yes, ma'am."

"I didn't know Betty had a nephew. Did you know that, Marge?" Carol asked the other woman.

"No. But I don't know Betty very well," Marge said.

"No, me neither," Carol quickly followed.

Considering how friendly Betty was and how small this town was, this surprised me. Maybe I lucked out. Maybe Betty's good-luck amulet was working.

"Well, I'll give Betty a call later and we'll straighten all this out," Carol said.

So much for luck.

"We'll put you in basic geometry," Carol said, "until we can test you."

"Great," I said quickly.

"Okay. And you would normally get to choose an elective, but most of them fill up so quickly that I can only offer you two choices," Carol said. "Computer Animation or Medieval Russian History?"

That was it? Computer Animation or Medieval Russian History. That's like asking a guy if he wants a punch to the face or a swift kick to the stomach. How about neither. I hated the thought of an animation class and, while I had been to Russia several times with my mom, I didn't care about their—or anyone else's—medieval history.

"Animation," I said meekly. "I guess."

"Oh, cheer up." Carol laughed. "You're going to love it."

"So, Finbar," Carol continued as she tapped on the keyboard, "we utilize the buddy system here in Galena."

"The buddy system?" I asked.

"Yeah, I'm going to pair you up with someone. They will take care of you while you make your transition. They will have all the same classes. Answer questions. Introduce you to people. That kind of stuff," she said, clacking away on the computer.

"Okay," I said, praying to God that she paired me with one particular sixteen-year-old girl with long dark hair and green eyes.

Carol finally stopped clicking and picked up the telephone. "Will Mike Marius please report to the office. Mike

Marius," she repeated. "Please report to the office."

I could hear her words bouncing off the hall walls outside the office.

"I'm going to pair you with Mike. He's a good kid and fairly new himself," she said. "He'll show you around and keep you safe." Then she winked.

Safe? What was Mike going to keep me safe from?

CHAPTER THIRTY-THREE

Mike came down to the office and actually seemed like a pretty good guy.

"So, where are you from?" Mike asked.

"All over," I said. "Mostly the East Coast, I guess."

"Cool. I've never been out of the Midwest. I'd love to see New York someday."

"Yeah, it's cool."

Mike gave me a tour of the school.

"So the office said you just moved to Galena too," I said, as we walked down a hallway toward the gym.

"Yeah, my mom, sister, and I moved up here from Chicago," Mike said.

Mike opened a door and we walked into the weight

room. It was huge. It had rows of weights and equipment and heavy bags and huge dudes.

"Man, this is nicer than most health clubs," I said.

"Yeah," Mike agreed. "This school is serious about their football. It's kind of annoying, actually. Two of the coaches are former Bears. They've got Super Bowl rings and everything."

"Great."

"Come on, we better get to first period. You don't want to be late for Nonnemacher."

"What class is Nonnemacher?" I asked, as we ran down the hall.

"Spanish."

"Great. I've only studied French and Italian."

"Sucks to be you," Mike said as we entered the classroom.

"*Hola, Señor Nonnemacher*," Mike said as we walked in the room.

"*Hola, Miguel. ¿Quién es tu amigo?*" Mr. Nonnemacher asked.

"Ah, what?" Mike asked as he walked toward the back of the room.

"I think he wants to know who I am," I said.

"Ah . . . *¿Habla usted español?*" Mr. Nonnemacher asked.

"No," I said, "but I do speak a little Italian and French."

"Oh, *si parla italiano!*" Nonnemacher said.

"*Sí.*"

I handed Nonnemacher the piece of paper the office had given me. I looked around the room. There were six or seven girls. Four of them were blond and three of them had darkish hair. One of the three had long hair and light eyes. Maybe she was the witness.

Nonnemacher handed me back the paper and said, "*Seguir adelante y tomar asiento en cualquier lugar.*"

"Sorry, I didn't get any of that."

"Have a seat anywhere you like, Mr. Jennings."

I took a seat in the last row next to Mike. I opened my notebook and tried to look like I was actually paying attention.

Nonnemacher started rambling in Spanish. I couldn't understand a word he said. Every few minutes, the entire class would all say a word out loud. And it went on like that for nearly twenty minutes. No one spoke a word of English the entire time, until class was just about over.

That's when my phone started ringing. That's when Nonnemacher brought out the English.

"Who is that?" he demanded. "Who is disturbing my class?"

The entire class was now looking at me as I tried to fish my phone out of my pocket. It was Emma calling.

"Bring me that phone, Mr. Jennings."

I pushed cancel and handed him my phone.

"Sorry about that," I said. Everyone was still looking at me.

"I don't know what kind of ill-mannered behavior your last school tolerated, but we do not allow cell phones here."

"Sorry, sir," I said again.

Nonnemacher put my phone in one of his desk drawers and started rambling in Spanish again until the bell rang.

I waited for the room to clear out, and then I approached him wearing the most apologetic look I could manage.

"I'm sorry about the phone thing," I said.

"I do not tolerate distractions in my class, Mr. Jennings."

"I understand. It won't happen again," I said.

"Good."

I stood still for several moments. Nonnemacher ignored me.

"Can I please have it back, sir?" I asked as politely as I could.

"At the end of the year."

"At the end of the year?" I asked. "You're kidding, right?"

Nonnemacher stopped what he was doing and looked up at me. He wasn't kidding.

"I don't kid," he said.

"My parents are still overseas. That phone is their only way of communicating with me," I lied.

"You should have thought of that before you brought it into my classroom."

I stood and stared at him. He just stared back. I could tell he wasn't going to budge. Should I just *take* the phone back?

What could he do, kick me out of a school I didn't actually attend? But I decided it was best not to push it too far. I needed to find the girl in the witness protection program, and getting kicked out would make that much harder.

I walked out into the hall. Mike was waiting for me.

"You're off to a good start. Can't wait to see who you'll piss off next." He laughed. "Man, I thought Nonnemacher was going to lose it when your phone went off. Did you see the look on his face?"

"He's a jerk," I said.

"Hanging with you is gonna be fun, Finbar." Mike punched me on the arm.

CHAPTER THIRTY-FOUR

*T*he rest of the morning was better. Not great, but better. Mike had a nutrition class, a business class, and geometry. I kept my mouth shut and stared down at my notebook during geometry.

We sat with a couple of Mike's friends at lunch. Some kid named Ben Hoyt, who seemed pretty cool. And a guy named Scott Cummings, who wouldn't stop talking about NASCAR. I ate a cheeseburger with fries and pudding. It was a little over six bucks. I was down to way under two hundred dollars now.

Maybe it was because I hadn't eaten a hot meal in days, but the cheeseburger tasted incredible.

"Whoa, slow down there, Fin, you're going to choke," Ben said.

"Dude, this is a good burger," I said.

"Where did you say you were from again?" Mike asked.

"The East Coast," I said.

"Didn't they have cheeseburgers on the East Coast?" Scott asked.

"Not this good," I said as I shoved the last piece of burger into my mouth.

"Oh, man! You guys should have seen Fin here with old man Nonnemacher."

"What happened?" Ben asked.

"It was no big deal," I said.

"Fin's phone goes off in the middle of class and I swear I could see that vein in Nonnemacher's forehead damn near pop."

"Sweet," Scott said.

"Yeah, but he took my phone."

"Oh, harsh. Was it a nice one?" Ben asked.

"No. It was a piece of junk," I said. "But now I've got to go buy another piece of junk. That'll be, like, my third phone in a week."

"Well, don't bring the new one into Watson's class. She took my iPhone last year, and I never got it back," Scott said.

"Dude, I don't think she can do that. That's stealing," Mike said.

"Well, she gave it back, but not to me," Scott added.

"What are you talking about?" Mike asked.

"The old bag gave it to my old man and he kept it. He still uses it. And I paid for it!"

Mike and Ben practically fell off the bench laughing. I guess I didn't find idiot fathers quite as funny.

"Hey, it's Famous Amos!" a female voice said. "Move over, dork."

The girl from the Piggly Wiggly was pushing Mike aside. Mike slid over and made room.

"What's with you?" Mike asked.

"Hey, how are you doing?" I asked Trish.

Mike looked shocked. "Do you two know each other?"

"Sure do." She didn't offer Mike any further explanation.

"Trish, right?" I asked. But I didn't need to ask; I could still see her name tag in my head.

"You've got a good memory, Amos."

She didn't know the half of it.

"How do you know my sister?" Mike asked.

"Your sister?"

"Yup. We're twins. Can't you see the resemblance?" Trish asked.

They looked nothing alike. Trish was gorgeous, in a dark and twisty kinda way, while Mike was, well, not dark and gorgeous.

"How do you know Finbar?" Mike asked again.

"What the heck is a Finbar?" Trish asked.

Before I realized what I was saying, I replied, "*I'm* a Finbar."

Trish lifted her eyebrows and made some sort of noise.

"We met at the Piggly Wiggly yesterday," I said.

"Oh." Mike went back to eating his tater tots.

"Trish was telling me how much she loves the cheerleaders here in Galena," I added.

"God. Don't get her started," Ben warned.

"What?" Trish asked innocently. "Look at them." She pointed to a table full of platinum blondes. "They're perfect. What's not to love?"

I was still looking at the cheerleaders. Not a bad-looking one in the bunch. All but two had blond hair.

"You like them cheerleader types, Amos?" Trish asked.

"No," I lied. "I'm just looking over at the table of football players. Do they always sit together?"

A group of huge guys were sitting at the table next to the cheerleaders. Their massive bodies dwarfed the lunch table.

"They do everything together," Ben said. "The coach thinks it builds some sort of bond."

"So what brings you to Galena, Amos?" Trish asked.

"My parents are in the military. They're overseas, so I'm staying here with my aunt for the next year."

"That's cool," Trish said. "I'd give anything to be overseas. Anywhere but this sewer."

"Not a fan of Galena?" I asked.

"How could you be a fan of this pathetic place? That's like asking if I'm a fan of pus-filled blisters. No one likes them, but sometimes you're forced to tolerate them."

CHAPTER THIRTY-FIVE

*T*he afternoon classes were much easier. Mike had a desktop publishing class and the 3-D Computer Animation class. Computer animation was clearly his thing.

"How did you get that spear in his hands?" I said, looking over Mike's shoulder at the scene he was creating.

"It just needs to sit farther down the z-axis than the outside of his hand."

"Right," I said as I looked at the bluish-black blob on my screen. Then I glanced back at Mike's. "Shut up, man! Now your guy is walking?"

"Well, Fin, it *is* an animation class," Mike said.

"For you, maybe." I couldn't draw a stick figure to save my life, and forget about making it walk.

I dragged my blob around the screen for the next fifty minutes while Mike's character was hunting woolly mammoth. The bell finally rang, putting me out of my misery.

"You're really good at that stuff," I said as we walked out of the computer lab.

"Thanks," Mike said. "Say, what are you doing tonight?"

"Nothing. I don't know a soul in this town."

"Do you want to come out to The Territories and hang out?"

"The Territories?"

"Yeah, it's where we live. It's a resort community thing just south of here. We've got horses and pools and stuff."

"Cool," I said. "How do I get there?"

Mike asked if I had a car. Now that my father was dead, I supposed I had technically inherited his many cars—including his red Ferrari. But it would be another four years before I would be old enough to drive it. Legally, anyway.

"No. Not here," I replied.

"I'll pick you up, then. You said your aunt runs Betty's Bluff Inn, right?"

"Yeah."

"Cool. How about six thirty?" Mike asked.

"Sounds good."

"Awesome. Bring your swimsuit and maybe we'll go up to the clubhouse. You never know, we might luck out and find Amanda and company up there."

"Who's Amanda and company?" I asked.

"The cheerleaders, silly."

"Okay." It looked like I had to shop for a swimsuit as well as a new phone.

I opened my notebook as I walked back toward the Pig. I had made a list of girls with long dark hair and light eyes who looked to be sixteen years old. There was the one girl in Nonnemacher's Spanish class. There were three girls in Mike's publishing class, two in his nutrition class, four in his math class, and four in his business ethics class. Not to mention the two brunettes at the cheerleader's table. That was a total of about sixteen girls who fit the description of the girl in my dad's book.

I managed to get most of their first names. But that was just for the girls I saw today. Essentially, just the girls in Mike's classes. How many other girls might fit the bill who weren't in his classes? And how was I going to check for green eyes? I was pretty sure I had freaked a couple of them out today with some extra-long stares. This wasn't going to be as easy as I'd thought.

I headed back to the Pig and bought the exact same phone I had purchased on Saturday. But this time I would make sure to shut it off before I walked into Nonnemacher's class. I also picked out a cheap red swimsuit, a box of crackers, a tub of spreadable port wine cheese, and two Mountain Dews. The bill was $62.43. That left me with only $120.59.

CHAPTER THIRTY-SIX

I *got back to Betty's around a quarter to five and was* shocked to see a police officer sitting with her at the table in the middle of the living room.

"Oh, there you are," Betty said as I walked through the door. She seemed a little nervous.

I wondered if somehow they had figured out who I was. Should I turn around and run? The cop was older and definitely overweight. I could easily outrun him.

"Are you enjoying Galena, Finbar?" Betty asked, still wearing a nervous look.

"I guess so," I said as I started to back up. The cop looked at me. He was in his late sixties. He had his hand stretched out across the table, and Betty was examining his palm with a magnifying glass.

"Fantastic," Betty said, and then they both looked back down at his palms.

The cop was just a customer. Thank goodness.

I walked up to the Second House and plugged in my new phone. It chirped to life. I pulled Emma's number out and dialed. No answer. I left her a message to call me and I explained I had to get a new phone.

I sat on my futon until 6:30 p.m. and then headed downstairs. Betty and the cop were gone. I sat out on the front porch and Mike pulled up in an old black Honda at about a quarter to seven.

"Sorry I'm late, dude."

"No worries," I said.

"Did you bring your suit?" Mike asked.

"Yeah."

"Cool," Mike said as he peeled away from the curb.

"So, Fin, are you a Yankees fan, being from New York and all?"

"No. I'm from the East Coast, but I've never actually lived in New York City itself. I'm a Twins fan."

"Oh, man!" Mike slammed on the brakes. "Dude, you're gonna have to walk it. I can't be letting no Twinkies fan in my car."

"Ah, let me guess—you're a White Sox guy?"

"Born and bred."

"Sucks to be you this year," I said.

Mike stepped on the gas again. "True that. Mauer smoked us right out of the playoffs."

"Yes, he did." I smiled.

"Did you see the game last night?"

"No. Betty doesn't have a TV."

"That sucks. I'd die. But your boys took it to New York pretty good," Mike said.

I thought about the Yankees and my grandpa. He was a huge Yankees fan. I thought about his funeral. I hoped someone took care of it. I hoped it was nice.

We sat in silence as Mike drove down Highway 20. We passed field after field of cows and horses. Mike turned off the highway about ten miles south of town. A giant waterfall and a sign welcomed us to The Territories. Golf courses lined both sides of the road.

"Nice," I said.

"Yeah, I like it here. We vacationed up here a couple of times when I was a kid," Mike said. "After my parents got divorced, my mom wanted to get out of Chicago and live in the country. I like it all right, but Trish has never really acccpted it."

"The divorce or Galena?" I asked.

"Oh, she accepted the divorce. It's Galena she hates."

"I think I could get used to it. It's gorgeous."

"We get a lot of celebrities up here in the summer. Michael Jordan's got a place here. But it's dead all winter. After the leaves fall, that's it for the year. There's just a handful of people that live out here year-round."

Mike pulled up to a large gate and pushed a button on the driver's-side visor.

"This is your house?"

"*Mi casa es su casa.*"

"I told you, I took French and Italian," I said.

Mike pulled in and parked next to a red beat-up Ford with an Illinois license plate that read SAME2U.

"Your sister's car?"

"How did you ever guess?"

As we walked inside, Mike yelled, "I'm home."

"Nice place," I said.

"Thanks. Make yourself at home. I'm just going to grab my suit and some towels."

I walked around looking at photos of Trish and Mike over the years.

"Fin, did you eat yet?" Mike called from down the hall.

"Not really," I yelled back.

"Well, if you're hungry we could grab something up at the clubhouse. They've got awesome burgers. I know how you like burgers."

I thought about my tub of cheese getting warm in the

Second House and yelled back, "Yeah, that would be—"

Trish walked out of nowhere, and I jumped.

"Yo, Amos."

"Hey," I said, trying not to look like a complete loser. "You scared the crap out of me."

"I have that effect," she said. "What are you doing?"

Mike walked in carrying a gym bag. "Hey, Trish. Want to come up to the clubhouse with us?"

"Are you serious?"

"Come on, I'm trying to show Fin here a good time."

"I'll pass. No offense, Fin, but I can't stand the people up there."

"You can't stand the people anywhere," Mike said.

"Not anywhere in this hick town," she replied.

Trish disappeared back down the hallway, and we hopped in Mike's car and drove up and down hills for what seemed like miles.

"This is a huge neighborhood," I said.

"Yeah, it's like seventy thousand acres. It's got three golf courses, horses, swimming pools . . . The Territories even has its own police force. Well, rent-a-cops."

We pulled up to a large chalet-style building on top of a hill. The parking lot was almost empty.

"Sorry, dude, looks like a quiet night. That's too bad—I was hoping to introduce you to some ladies."

"No worries."

Mike and I had dinner in the club's bar. I had a cheese-burger. I hoped it would be as good as the one at school. And it was. Better, even. Then we shot a couple games of pool. Mike insisted on playing for cash. I wasn't thrilled about the idea but, fortunately for me, Mike sucked at pool, and my cash supply was back over $200 by the time we finished.

"Do you want to go for a dip?"

"Sure. Why not."

Mike led the way to the men's locker room. We put our suits on and walked out to a massive indoor pool. There were four guys and two girls sitting on the far edge of the pool. The guys were huge. Football players, I guessed.

"Ah, man," Mike whispered.

"What?"

"Duane and his buddies. They don't usually come out here."

"Do they live in The Territories?" I asked.

"No way! They're townies. Amanda lives out here, though."

"Which one is Amanda?" I asked.

"The smoking hot one sitting next to Duane."

That didn't help. Both girls were smoking hot. And both were sitting next to the biggest of the four guys. I assumed he was Duane.

"Is Amanda the blonde or the brunette?" I asked.

"The blonde," Mike said. "The brunette is a new girl named Bailey."

I set my towel down on the table and tried to look relaxed. I turned my back to the football players.

"We can't leave, Mike," I said. "They've already seen us."

Mike started to say something, but I knew it was too late. I could already hear Duane yelling something across the pool. I hated guys like Duane. And I had met many Duanes over the years. Thick-headed, slow-talking Neanderthals who lived to show off for their buddies. And over the years, I found there was only one way to deal with guys like Duane. I hoped I was wrong, but I had a strong feeling tonight wouldn't end well. For Duane, at least.

He was yelling something across the pool. His voice was echoing. I could only make out some of the words. But I was certain I heard the words "new buddy" and "girlfriend."

Mike yelled something back and now Duane was walking to us.

"What did you say, Windy?" Duane yelled back.

"Wendy?" I asked.

"Windy. That's what he calls us—Trish and me. Because we're from Chicago."

Now Duane was a few feet away.

"Oh, I get it, *windy*. Like the Windy City," I said.

"Who's your girlfriend?" Duane asked without looking

in my direction. The brunette, Bailey, was now halfheartedly trying to call Duane off.

"Duane!" Bailey called. "Duane, get back here before I get bored and go home."

Before I could stop him, I heard Mike say, "Finbar is new to Galena."

Oh god, that was the worst thing he could say. Not only was I the new guy, which meant Duane would probably feel like he had to challenge me, especially in front of girls, but to make matters worse, my name was Finbar. That combo was certain death. I knew guys like Duane and he wasn't going to let that go. Ever. God, I hated my fake name.

Duane was now looking at me.

"Finbar? What kind of girly name is Finbar?" he asked.

"Irish," I said. "And I agree, it is a bad name."

"A *girly* name." He repeated.

I looked Duane up and down. I was a big guy, for a *twelve*-year-old, but Duane was a monster. A beast.

"Hey, man. We don't want any trouble. This is my first day here. I'm just hanging out," I said.

But I knew that wouldn't work. Duane had a look of shock on his face. I was certain he wasn't used to anyone actually responding to his comments.

"I'm leaving, Duane," Bailey yelled as she pulled her Blackhawks sweatshirt over her swimsuit.

I glanced at Amanda. She was still sitting with Duane's

buddies. She seemed to be enjoying the show.

"Look," I said to Duane, "I don't want to upset you, and this is a really big pool." I motioned with my hands to indicate that the pool was truly massive. "How about Mike and I hang out here for a little bit"—I motioned to a small section of the shallow end—"and you guys use the rest of the pool. We're not staying long," I added.

"We're using the entire pool now," Duane said loud enough for his buddies to hear. "You girls can use it after we're done."

I looked over at Mike. He looked absolutely terrified. I'd been in this situation more times than I could remember. Every school had a guy like Duane. Sometimes several guys like Duane. And they always had to screw with the new guy.

My mom had encouraged me to be the "smarter man" and walk away. Which now seemed funny, given her occupation. But walking away never worked. In fact, it got worse 100 percent of the time. My dad understood that.

We saw my dad in Greece one time just after a group of older boys had kicked the crap out of me. It was the first time I had really seen my dad angry. And over the course of his visit, he told me to never back down from the initial test. He told me to find the biggest, baddest guy in the group and take him down first. And take him down hard. He guaranteed me that the others would back away. And he was right. It worked 100 percent of the time. But the biggest and baddest guys weren't usually *this* big and bad. And they weren't usually in high school. I was used to dealing with guys my own age. I thought I'd try reasoning with Duane one more time.

"Look." I forced a smile on my face and took a step toward Duane. "We're going to swim down on this end of the pool, and you guys can have that end." I didn't wait for a response. I just started taking off my shirt to show him I was serious. And that's when it started. And it wasn't just Duane, it was his buddies and Amanda, too. They were all laughing. And pointing. I looked down at my chest. Betty's giant blue eye was hanging around my neck. I'd forgotten all about it.

I grabbed the giant eye by the corner and tilted it up so I could see it better. "Yeah, I admit it's a little weird," I said.

"*You're* a little weird, FIN-BAR," Duane said, poking at the amulet.

"Duane, you're acting like a jerk." Bailey was walking toward us now, but Duane ignored her.

"Leave him alone, Duane," Mike said.

"Oh, is FIN-BAR from *windy*-town too?"

"Oh." I laughed. "I get it, the Windy City—funny."

"Your friend's a jerk," Duane said as he grabbed the front of Mike's shirt.

"I wouldn't do that if I were you," I said.

"Oh, really?" Duane twisted his massive fists and Mike's shirt looked like it was now cutting into his neck.

"Let him go," I demanded.

"Make me." He twisted harder. Mike was turning red. Bailey was standing next to Duane now. She looked like she was going to cry.

"Stop it!" she shouted.

I let go of the giant eye amulet, stepped toward Duane, and decided to borrow a line from my dad's book.

"Let go or they'll be picking pieces of you out of the pool filter for the next month." It didn't seem to faze him. I guess it sounded better in my dad's book. Duane just twisted harder and started to lift Mike off the ground.

I tilted my head back, like I was gesturing toward the door behind me, like I was going to suggest that Mike and I just leave. Then I snapped my head forward as fast and hard as I could, smashing my forehead into Duane's nose. I felt his nose give way. I could hear it crunch as it broke into several pieces. His face exploded in a bloody mess. The force and shock of the blow caused Duane to let go of Mike and stagger several steps, falling into the pool with a loud splash. Within seconds, both of his buddies were in the water, swimming to his aid. Bailey and Amanda were both yelling. Duane let out a string of expletives and threats.

"We'd better go," Mike said.

"Probably," I agreed.

Mike was now beyond terrified. He was wringing his hands and mumbling all the way to the car. He was on the verge of tears. His hands were shaking so badly by the time we reached the car that he could hardly open the door.

"It's okay," I said, trying to calm him down. But I was starting to feel sick myself. Adrenaline always made me nauseated.

"Fin, you're a dead man."

"I don't think so. Usually these guys avoid me after."

"After?" Mike asked. "You've done this before?"

"A couple of times. You'd be amazed at how hard your forehead is. It's an old trick my dad taught me."

"You don't know Duane. Your dad doesn't know Duane. And you don't know the football team. They're all for one and one for all, that kind of stuff. They'll all come after you."

"Seriously. I'll be okay," I said. I was actually more worried about Mike's ability to drive than Duane and his buddies.

CHAPTER THIRTY-SEVEN

Mike was a little calmer by the time we got to the highway.

"Man! That was terrifying. You're a crazy man! And a dead man! Oh, wait until I tell Trish. She hates Duane more than I do."

I was about to comment when my phone rang. I fished it out of my pocket. My hand was shaking from the adrenaline. I switched the phone to my right hand so Mike wouldn't notice.

"Hello?"

"Hey," Emma said. "Are you okay? You sound kind of funny."

"Yeah," I lied. "I'm good. What's up with you?"

"I'm just on break and got your message. Why did you get a new phone?" Emma asked.

"Well," I said honestly, "the Spanish teacher here in Galena took mine."

Mike looked over at me and yelled out, "Nonnemacher!"

"Who was that?"

"That's Mike," I said.

"Are you okay?" Emma asked.

"I'm fine," I replied. "I'll call you first thing in the morning."

"Okay. Please take care of yourself."

I agreed I would and hung up as Mike sped up the bluff in his crappy Honda.

"Hey, do you want a ride to school tomorrow? After what you did to Duane, I'm not sure you should be walking around town alone."

I accepted the ride, but it wasn't out of fear. Experience told me Duane was going to be in way too much pain to go to school tomorrow. Or any day this week.

CHAPTER THIRTY-EIGHT

I *laid on my futon thinking about Bailey, wondering if* she could be the witness protection girl I was looking for. I circled and starred her name on my list of dark-haired, green-eyed girls. I needed to get close to Bailey. But first, I closed my eyes and fell asleep.

My head was pounding when I woke up. I half expected to see a massive bruise across my forehead from where I'd smacked Duane, but it actually didn't look too bad. A little red and a little swollen, but I was sure Duane was looking in the mirror and seeing much worse.

I put on my last clean T-shirt and brushed my teeth. There was another copy of the *Galena Gazette* under my door. The front page had a large photo of someone I recognized immediately. It was a photo of Attorney General Como with a caption under it that read: NEXT PRESIDENT?

I threw the newspaper on the floor next to the futon and headed downstairs. It was 7:35 and Mike wasn't here yet. It was cold this morning. I could kiss my billiards winnings good-bye if I had to buy a jacket. I could kiss *food* good-bye if I had to buy a jacket.

A car pulled up a few minutes later. The license plate read SAME2U. It was Trish.

"Hey, where's Mike?" I asked as I climbed into the car.

"Well, it's nice to see you, too."

"Hey, Trish," I said. "Sorry, I was just expecting your brother."

"The putz is just running late, as usual. I told him there was no sense in making you late too." Trish peeled away from the curb.

"Thanks," I said.

"It was cool, what you did for Mike. Standing up to Duane," Trish said.

"I just hope they don't take it out on Mike later."

"What about you? Aren't you worried about what they will do to you?" Trish asked.

"No. Not really. I've met a lot of guys like Duane. They usually stay away once you lay down the ground rules," I said.

"I wouldn't have pegged you for such a tough guy," Trish said as she sped down Main Street.

I braced myself against her dashboard. "Whoever

taught you and your brother to drive should be arrested."

"It's the Chicago way, baby."

Trish kept her foot on the gas and the engine continued to roar. She must have been going twenty miles over the speed limit as she rounded the corner just outside of town.

"Watch it!" I yelled.

She slammed on her brakes when she saw the sea of flashing lights. It looked like the entire Galena police force had pulled over six or seven semi trucks. One of the officers stepped out into the highway and motioned for Trish to come to a complete stop.

"What are you thinking, Trish?" he yelled as he walked around to the driver's-side door. "You could've killed someone going that fast. You could have killed me," the officer said.

"Sorry, Sheriff," Trish said. "It won't happen again."

"It better not."

"What's going on here?"

"Oh, some trucks left the Happy Puppy Dog Food Company carrying some bad freight." The sheriff rubbed his eyes and said, "Slow down, ya hear?" And he walked away.

"All these cops for bad freight?" I asked.

"Gotta be drugs," Trish said as she stepped on the gas. "Or someone hijacked a truck full of stuff that didn't belong to them."

"Is that what they did back in Chicago?" I asked. "Is that the Chicago way?"

"You know it!"

CHAPTER THIRTY-NINE

Not only was I now late for school, but I had no idea where I was supposed to go. I had blindly followed Mike around the previous day and hadn't paid attention to classroom numbers. I hadn't even paid attention to what floor we had been on for each class.

Trish went off to her class, and I sat by Mike's locker hoping he would show up before a teacher started questioning me. Five minutes later, Mike came running down the hall.

"Dude, I'm so sorry. Trish picked you up, right?"

"Yeah," I said. "I just wasn't sure where I was supposed to be."

Mike looked at his watch. "There's only, like, five minutes of Spanish left. Nonnemacher is going to kill us."

I had no desire to see Nonnemacher again. "Why don't we just skip Spanish and head to the next class?"

"Okay," Mike agreed. "Probably best. He really hates it when you come in late. If we walked in now, I think his head would explode."

Mike threw his jacket into his locker, grabbed a few books, and slammed the door shut.

"What's after Spanish?" I asked.

"Nutrition," Mike said.

Nutrition. Perfect. Mike's class with Bailey.

"Are you worried about Duane?" Mike asked.

"No," I said honestly. I figured there was a good chance Duane would be out the whole week. A busted nose might not be life-threatening, but it hurt like crazy. And your face looks god-awful for weeks.

"I wonder if we should eat outside today," Mike said. "I mean, there's no reason to chum the waters by sitting near the football table. Maybe we could even run over to McDonald's for lunch."

"Trust me, I'll be fine. Duane doesn't seem like the kind of guy who would want his buddies standing up for him. He'll want to take revenge himself. If he does anything at all. I told you, these guys usually go away quietly."

"I've never seen Duane do anything quietly," Mike said.

I wanted to change the subject. "So tell me about Bailey."

"Bailey? What's to tell? She's hot, smart, and part of Amanda's crew."

"Is she a cheerleader too?" I asked.

"They are all cheerleaders. She and Amanda live on the same block out in The Territories. She just moved a little while ago."

"Is she friends with Duane?"

"I don't know. I've seen her with a couple of the players. Like I said, just stay away, Fin. Don't chum the waters."

I said nothing and we walked into the classroom as the first bell rang.

Mr. Metzel was sitting behind his desk.

"Ah, Mr. Marius and—it's Jennings, right? Mr. Jennings?"

"Yes, sir," I replied.

"How are you gentleman doing today?" Metzel asked.

"Good," Mike said. I didn't say anything, I just took a seat in the back row. Bailey was one of the last to come in. She sat in front of Mike.

"Good. Well, yesterday we were talking about cholesterol. Who can tell me about cholesterol?" Metzel asked. No one said a word. I stared down at my notebook.

"Is cholesterol good or bad?"

"Both?" someone said. "Right? Didn't you say it could be good and bad?"

"Correct, Robby. There are two kinds of cholesterol, right? One's good and one is bad. Does anyone remember which one is good?"

A girl in the front row raised her hand.

"Yes, Darcy."

"Is it DHL?" she asked.

"Close," Metzel said. "It's HDL. DHL is a delivery service. But that's good, Darcy. Has anyone ever been to a large city like Cedar Rapids or Des Moines and seen the yellow DHL delivery vans?"

Metzel paused and no one said a thing. I continued to stare at my notebook.

"The DHL vans are delivering goods, right? Just like HDL is delivering good cholesterol. Thank you, Darcy. That's a good way to remember HDL in case that appears on a test someday. Hint. Hint."

Metzel went on and on about HDL, LDL, triglycerides, and who knows what else for the next forty minutes. I might as well have been in Nonnemacher's Spanish class. I had no idea what he was talking about. I was about to nod off when Metzel began counting the number of students in the class. That meant some sort of group project. Maybe I'd catch a break and end up with Bailey.

He went up and down the rows, assigning people numbers between one and nine. Bailey was a six. I was a seven. But Mike was a six.

"Switch with me, Mike," I said.

"What? Why?"

"Please."

"Fine. What number are you?"

"I'm a seven," I said.

Metzel addressed the class and told the various groups to meet in different parts of the room. The sixes were meeting at the front of the room. I walked to the front and sat next to Bailey. There was one other girl in our group.

"Okay, class. Here is the assignment. Each group will prepare a heart-friendly good cholesterol dish to share with the entire class on Thursday. You need to write up the recipe and describe why you believe the dish to be heart-friendly, okay? Pick one person to speak for the group on Thursday."

The class let out a collective moan.

"Please take the last few minutes of class to discuss with your teammates."

I turned toward Bailey and the other girl.

"Hey, my name's Fur—" Whoa, I almost said Furious. "Finbar," I said quickly.

"Oh, I know who you are," Bailey said. "Everyone knows who you are."

"How is that? I just started yesterday." This was going to be harder than I thought.

"Quite a first day," Bailey said. "Breaking Duane's nose and all."

"You were there last night, weren't you?" I pretended not to remember her. Or her swimsuit. "You know, I didn't mean to break it. I just wanted him to back off."

Bailey said. "It sure looked like you tried to break it. You got blood on my new swimsuit."

"I really didn't try. But I didn't not try either. I get the feeling subtlety might not have worked with Duane."

"Well, you're probably right about that," Bailey agreed.

"I'll say," the other girl added.

"I didn't catch your names," I said.

"I'm Susan." She held out her hand.

"I'm Bailey."

"Well, Susan and Bailey, what are we going to cook for Thursday?"

CHAPTER FORTY

*T*he bell rang before we could talk about our heart-friendly recipe options. I tried to follow Bailey down the hall, but Mike was heading in the opposite direction.

"I wouldn't have switched," Mike said, "if I'd known what you were up to. That's not cool, dude. Not cool at all."

"What?"

"Why Bailey? Duane will kill you if he sees you with Bailey."

"Look at her," I said. We both looked down the hall and watched Bailey walk away. "Why not Bailey? Besides, you already said Duane was going to kill me. I might not have your computer and math skills, Mike, but I know he can't possibly kill me twice."

"You don't even know her, dude," Mike said.

"I don't know anyone here."

"I'm begging you, Fin, just lay low. You don't know these guys. You just got here, man; I'd hate to see you die too soon," Mike said. "I mean, you're kind of like my personal bodyguard after last night." Mike punched me on the arm.

"Okay. Okay."

The rest of the morning was uneventful. I sat and listened to teachers I knew I'd never see again after Thursday. I hated school when I actually had to be there. It was even worse when I didn't.

Mike's friends Ben and Scott came running up as soon as we walked into the lunchroom.

"Dude! Is it true?" Scott was jumping up and down.

I didn't have to ask what he was talking about, but I did. "Is what true?"

"Did you really bust Duane's nose?"

"I guess so," I said.

"Whoa!"

The entire lunchroom seemed to be staring in our, or my, direction. So much for laying low.

"Aren't you a little worried?" Ben asked. "Don't get me wrong, you're a tall guy and clearly you can handle yourself, but Duane—he's a monster."

"Why does everyone insist on reminding me how big and mean Duane is?" I snapped. "I know how big he is."

"Cool," Ben said. "I'm sorry."

"It's just—let's just talk about something else, okay?"

No one said a word as we went through the food line. I ordered a cheeseburger with tater tots and chocolate pudding. Why mess with a good thing?

We were walking toward the table we had sat at the day before when I noticed Bailey sitting with Amanda.

"I'll be right back," I told Mike as I headed toward Bailey. I could feel the eyes of the entire football team, minus Duane, home in on me as I crossed the lunchroom. I could see their thick necks all turning in unison as I stood next to Bailey.

"I'm thinking we should get the recipe for these cheeseburgers. You know, for our project. These things are amazing."

"Hey, Finbar," Bailey said, looking surprised to see me.

"Can I sit down?" I asked.

Maybe it was my apparent lack of fear, but she was now staring at me, speechless.

"We could discuss the cheeseburger and the UPS truck and whatever."

"It was DHL, not UPS," she said as she slid over. "And I don't think a cheeseburger has *good* cholesterol in it," she said.

I sat down.

"What are you doing?" Amanda demanded.

"Just talking with Bailey, here," I said.

"I see that. Bailey was there last night. She knows what you did."

I motioned around the room. "I think everyone knows what I did."

I glanced over at the football table. No one was eating. All their eyes were focused on me. I turned back toward Bailey.

"So, I don't know the first thing about cooking."

"I do," she said. "I'm Italian. My mom and I used to cook together all the time."

"Cool. So I'll manage the project, and you and Susan can do all the work."

"Manage the project?" Bailey mocked. "Yeah, right. I'll manage the project and you'll do all the cooking."

"You do realize that the entire football team is staring at you right now, right?" Amanda interjected.

"I thought they were looking at you," I said.

"Ah, I'm pretty sure they're looking at you," Amanda said.

I looked at the players' table and back at Bailey. "I think she might be right. Well, I'm going to go and talk to the chef about getting this burger recipe," I said as I stood up. I figured I was pushing my luck to stay much longer. "Who knows, maybe we'll luck out and the burgers will be tofu or something."

"I doubt it," Bailey said.

"One more thing, where and when are we going to cook this stuff?" I asked.

"We can do it at my house tomorrow after school," Bailey replied. "If that's okay with you and Susan."

"Works for me."

I walked back to Mike's table.

"You must have a death wish," Mike said. "You're not exactly popular with the football team or the cheerleaders, Fin."

"I know I'm not winning any popularity contests at this school."

"I don't know—Bailey looked like she was smiling the whole time," Ben said. "I've got to give you credit, Fin, you don't seem to have an ounce of fear in you."

"Or brains," Mike added.

I had plenty of fear, just nothing left to lose.

"So what do you guys do for fun on Tuesday nights around here?" I asked.

"There's lots to do. Have you been up to Dubuque yet? They've got a bowling alley up there," Scott said.

"Bowling, huh?"

"Yeah." Scott was excited now. "Who doesn't love bowling?"

"Right," I said. "How far is Dubuque?"

"Sixteen miles."

"Well, that's, like, six minutes if Mike drives."

"True. True," Scott said.

"Count me in," Mike said. "You never know what's going to happen when you're around, Finny."

"Hey, I'm keeping a low profile. Nothing is going to happen tonight."

"Sure," Mike said.

"Why don't we all meet in the parking lot of the Piggly Wiggly at seven," I said, figuring I could get dinner before we bowled.

Mike and I got up and headed to our Computer Animation class.

I sat and watched Mike work on his animation for almost an hour, and then Mike dropped me off at Betty's after school.

"See you at seven," I said.

CHAPTER FORTY-ONE

I *said good-bye to Mike and was halfway up Betty's* sidewalk when I noticed the living room curtain close quickly. Was someone watching me? Was it Betty? Or someone from school? Maybe the school had finally called Betty.

I opened the door slowly, not sure what to expect. I stepped inside and found Betty alone at the table in the middle of the living room.

"Finbar, there you are."

"Hey, Betty."

"Come. Come. Have a seat." She motioned to the seat across the table from her.

I sat down.

"So, how is your day going?" she asked.

"Good. Thanks," I said. I hoped she wasn't going to try and sell me some magic potions or healing services. I couldn't even afford potato chips at the Piggly Wiggly right now.

"Finbar." Betty pulled out a clipboard full of paper from beneath the table. "I've been doing some work on your chart. And, well, I'm confused. Maybe I'm just getting too old."

"No," I said, having absolutely no idea what we were talking about.

"It was your colors that originally concerned me the other day, dear. You're dark. Awfully dark. And I know you didn't ask, but I went ahead and read your cards, which is extremely difficult to do without you there." She squirmed in her chair. "And, obviously, at no charge to you. I was just concerned."

"Okay." I still had no idea what was going on. Betty had the same sympathetic look that the cop in New Canaan had when my grandpa told me my dad had died.

"I'm usually pretty good at reading the cards, but I've made mistakes, you see."

"Yeah," I said.

She pulled a tarot card out of her stack of paper and placed it on the table. It depicted a man with a rope around one foot. The man was hanging upside down. The man didn't appear to be in pain. He was just sort of hanging there. I guess I didn't find it as upsetting as Betty.

"The hanging man," Betty whispered.

"Okay," I said.

"Well, naturally I was concerned," she said.

"What does it mean?"

"It can have lots of meanings. It all depends."

"I'm getting the feeling none of them are good," I said.

"Under certain circumstances it could signify a martyr. Or some sort of sacrifice. It could also signify a person stuck or suspended."

"Suspended?"

"Maybe suspended between good and evil. Or between death and life."

"Aren't we all?" I joked. Betty didn't laugh.

"But there is good news. Like I said, I have been wrong before. So I went to the books and checked some less orthodox methods of divination."

Betty pulled out more paper from her clipboard and placed them on the table. "Based on your birthday and time, your charts look good. And I even looked into onomancy, and everything turns up roses, you see."

"Onomancy?" I asked.

"Yes, I know it sounds farfetched," she said, and then quickly added, "and I would never solely rely on the study of one's name, but it was a check and balance."

"Study of my name. I see."

"But Finbar, I'd like to ask a favor, just to appease this old lady. I would like to read your hands. It's really the only way to be certain."

"A palm reading?" I asked. Would she be able to tell I was lying from my palm?

"Yes," she said. "Free of charge, of course. I just need to know everything is all right. I need to know the card was— that I was wrong."

"Sure." I placed my right hand on the table. I felt bad tricking Betty. Clearly she knew something wasn't right. Maybe I'd tell her the truth after all of this was over so she didn't question her cosmic abilities.

"Both hands, dear."

Betty spent the next hour examining my hands. And I could tell she didn't like what she saw. She just kept sighing and saying, "Oh, dear. Oh, dear."

It was almost six o'clock when my phone started to ring. I pulled my right hand away from Betty.

"I'm sorry, I need to get that." I stood up and stepped out onto the porch. It was Emma.

"I can't tell you how glad I am that you called," I said as I walked up High Street, away from Betty and her prying eyes.

CHAPTER FORTY-TWO

Hey, Emma," I said, suddenly realizing I'd never called her back last night. "Sorry I didn't call you back last night. I was exhausted and fell asleep."

"I was worried about you," she said.

I smiled as I walked toward the bluff stairs. It was nice to have someone worrying about me.

"No worries," I said. "I've just been playing undercover detective and couldn't talk when you called."

"Can you tell me more about this big story? Did you find the proof you were looking for?" Emma asked.

I thought about Bailey and said, "Yeah, I think I've found the proof."

"What's the story?"

"I believe the Chicago gang task force has been dumping all of their witness protection people into Galena."

"What?"

"Yeah. And someone—who knows, maybe the sheriff here—tipped off the Mafia, and they are here killing the witnesses."

"That's crazy, Furious," Emma said. "There is almost no violence in Galena."

"Well, that's not really true: My mom was killed here. But now they're making the murders look like accidents."

"Your mom? That's where your mom was killed? In Galena? How do you know?"

"My dad wrote all about it in his new book. Same names. Same murders. Everything. It's a long story, Emma. But you have to trust me. It's all true."

"And you have proof of all this?"

"I think so. I'm still working on it. I'll call you tomorrow," I said.

CHAPTER FORTY-THREE

It was a little after six. I had plenty of time to walk to the Pig and get something to eat before the guys got there. I took Main Street to the highway and headed north. It took me about twenty minutes to get to the Pig. Trish was working.

"Hey, Amos, whatcha up to?"

I grabbed a Coke and a Snickers and walked to her checkout lane.

"Hey, Trish. I'm just grabbing a little dinner before I go bowling with your brother."

She glanced down at the Coke and Snickers.

"I don't know how you got so tall eating like this," she said as she scanned the items. "Is your dad tall?"

"He was," I said. "He's dead now."

"Crap, Amos, I'm sorry. Was he a good guy?"

I thought about my dad profiting from my mom's secret. I thought about the divorce and how sad my mom had been for such a long period of time. And then I thought about this town and his new book. And how he died trying to do the right thing.

"More or less," I answered.

"You're lucky," she said. "My dad's dead too. But he wasn't a good guy. Three eighty."

That was odd. Mike had made it sound like they moved to Galena after his parents had divorced. "When did he die?" I asked.

"A few months ago. Right before we moved to this butt-scab town."

Trish handed me my change and said, "Thanks for shopping the Pig."

I held up the Snickers and said, "I'm going to eat my dinner before your brother gets here."

"Have fun. Try not to break any bones over in Dubuque."

"I'll try."

I walked outside and sat down on the curb. I took a few swigs of my Coke and wondered if Mike, Trish, and their mom were in the witness protection program too. It made sense. Maybe a mobster killed Trish's dad and her mom testified in court. Maybe the state moved them here so they would be safe.

I took the last swig of Coke as a car pulled directly in front of me. I squinted as the headlights shined into my face. I couldn't see inside, but the car looked too big to be Mike's. And I thought Ben said he had a truck. Maybe it was Scott. I stood up to throw away the Snickers wrapper and Coke can. I looked into the car. It wasn't Scott. Or Ben. It was an older man. It was Director Douglas of the CIA.

CHAPTER FORTY-FOUR

Douglas was staring at me.

I didn't move.

What should I do?

How did he find me?

He kept staring at me. Neither one of us moved.

I needed to go. Now.

There was no way I was going to let him take me.

Douglas was slowly removing his seat belt.

Which direction should I run?

Left. I should run left. It would force Douglas to get out and have to run around the car.

I pushed off with my right foot. A half second later I was in a full sprint. I figured it would take Douglas a second to get the seat belt completely off. Another second to get out of the car. Then maybe two or three seconds to get around the car and give chase. Given our age and size difference, a four- or five-second head start was all I needed.

But I was wrong.

Douglas didn't get out of the car. He took half a second to throw the car into reverse. Another second to back up. And a fraction of a second to shift into drive.

I could practically smell the rubber as he stepped on the gas. He was closing in fast. I ran faster, but there was no way I was going to outrun the car. I needed a new plan.

I looked back. Douglas was screaming something. He didn't appear to be slowing down. I ran up onto the side- walk and stopped behind a brick pillar. The car's weight and momentum took Douglas twenty feet past me before he came to a complete stop. I took off running. *Where can I hide?* I heard a car door open. Douglas was now on foot. *Should I run out onto the highway? If someone saw Douglas chasing me, would they help me?* Douglas was with the CIA. He had a badge. There was no way anyone would stop him.

Maybe Trish could help. At least I could tell her that Douglas was crooked. Maybe she could tell someone. Maybe she could get me help.

I stepped in front of the Pig's automatic door. It was tak- ing forever to open. I pushed the door and ran inside. Trish was gone. No one was around. No employees. No customers. The store was empty.

"Trish!" I yelled.

Nothing. Where was she?

I started toward her register.

"Trish!"

I ducked down and crawled under the conveyer belt. My heart was pounding in my ears. I thought I heard the automatic door open. I was dead. There was no way out of this. I tried to hold my breath, and my chest felt like it was going to explode. He had to hear me. I let out a deep breath as quietly as I could. I could now hear Douglas's dress shoes clicking on the polished linoleum. Which way was he walking?

It sounded like the steps were getting farther away. I crawled out and peered over the cash register. Douglas was halfway down one of the aisles. I stood up and bolted for the door.

Douglas heard me and started running toward the door too. I was probably twenty feet closer to it than he was, but I had to stop and wait for the stupid automatic door to open.

Come on! Come on!

Douglas was now ten feet away.

"Stop, Furious!"

The door opened and I sprinted down the sidewalk. Douglas's car was directly in front of me. The car door was still open, and the engine was running. Could I steal the car?

I had never really driven before. My grandpa used to let me drive his squad car on the country roads of New Canaan, but he was always right there with me.

I looked back—he was fast. I didn't have a choice. I had to steal the car.

I jumped off the curb and ran for the car. I slid into the front seat, slammed the door shut, and stomped on the gas. And the engine revved, but the car didn't move. *Crap!* Douglas was now just a few feet away. I slid the center lever to DRIVE, and the car started to roll. Douglas was now pounding on the rear window. I stomped on the gas again, and the car raced forward. I checked the rearview mirror as I sped across the parking lot. Douglas was bent over, catching his breath. I kept the gas pedal to the floor as I pulled out onto the highway. The tires screeched as I jerked the car hard right to avoid hitting a crappy old Honda. It was Mike.

CHAPTER FORTY-FIVE

My hands were shaking as I drove down the highway toward downtown Galena. This entire thing kept getting worse. Now I was a car thief. It seemed like there was no way out of this mess. If I got caught now, I would go to jail. And then Douglas would take me. And probably kill me. Maybe Betty was right: Maybe I was the hanging man. Maybe this thing was going to end real badly.

I slowed down to ten miles under the speed limit. I needed to ditch the car quickly. I turned left onto Main Street and decided to park in the alley behind Dirty Gert's. It was dark and out of the way. Maybe the car would go unnoticed for a couple of days. Hopefully, I'd be long gone by the time someone found it.

I pulled up next to a Dumpster and left the keys in the ignition.

I jogged down Main Street to the bluff stairs. It was almost eight o'clock when I reached Betty's. No one was around. I went directly to the Second House and closed my door.

Now that Douglas knew I was in Galena, I wondered how long it would take him to find me here. Galena was a tourist town with lots of inns. And I had used a fake name. And Betty didn't seem to be too technologically advanced. She used a clipboard instead of a computer. There would be nothing for the CIA or FBI to track. I figured I was probably safe for now.

My phone rang. It was Emma, but I didn't feel like talking. I just lay on the futon for a couple of hours thinking about my dad. Trying to figure out what I should do next. And what I would do once the book came out. If I didn't find Anton before the book came out on Thursday, he would disappear. Would I have to spend the rest of my life looking over my shoulder? And where would I live? I had no friends or relatives to live with. I supposed I had a lot of money now, from my dad. But even if I survived Douglas and Anton, would the government let a twelve-year-old kid have the money? And they certainly wouldn't let me live alone. I would have to live somewhere and go to school somewhere.

How was I going to get out of this mess? My grandpa had said that Dad had even reached out to some of his powerful friends and they weren't able to help him. If the Salvatore crime syndicate had truly infiltrated organizations like the CIA, how was I going to stop them? How was I going to stop Douglas? How was I ever going to be safe?

I sat up and looked around the room. The adrenaline rush from running from Douglas and stealing his car had left me starving, even after having eaten my Snickers bar, but I didn't want to risk leaving. I looked down on the floor and picked up the *Galena Gazette*. Maybe there would be an ad for pizza. I could order a pizza and not have to leave.

I glanced through the paper, but the only mention of pizza was Cannova's. Cannova's was the place where Jimmy the British assassin-for-hire had worked. It was probably best to just go hungry.

I set the newspaper back down and noticed the photo of Attorney General Como on the front.

Maybe Como could help. He was a powerful man. I could call Como and tell him that I needed help. I could tell him that the Salvatore crime syndicate was behind my mom's, dad's, and grandpa's murders. I could tell him they had a crooked CIA agent. And I could tell him I had proof. Which I was hoping was true. If Bailey was who I thought she was.

I pulled out my phone and did a search for Attorney General Como. The Attorney General had a Web page at the Department of Justice. I clicked on the Contact Us button and called the phone number. I figured there would be no one in his office this time of night and the odds of me getting through to him were extremely slim, but I thought I'd try. I could leave a message that was detailed enough that some- one might feel compelled to actually give it to him. I clicked on the phone number and it began to dial.

There was a generic voice asking me to leave my message and someone from the justice office would follow up. I left a message.

"Hello, my name is Furious Jones. I am a friend of Attorney General Como and the son of Robert Jones. I was with the attorney general the night my father was killed and I would very much like to speak to him. I'm currently in Galena, Illinois, and I have information regarding the mur- ders of both my parents."

I left my phone number and asked that Como get in touch with me as soon as possible. I figured that was a mes- sage that would be difficult for an assistant to ignore.

CHAPTER FORTY-SIX

I *woke up a little late, brushed my teeth, and smelled* my T-shirts to see which one I could still wear. Today's *Galena Gazette* was under my door. The newspaper featured a photo of the Happy Puppy Dog Food Company and a headline reading: GRISLY DISCOVERY IN GALENA FACTORY. I threw the paper on the floor next to the newspaper with Como's picture on it. I was running late for school and didn't have time to read about Anton's latest kill.

I opened the door and peered out into the hallway. Betty wasn't around. I felt bad about walking out on Betty's palm reading yesterday, but I didn't have time for that stuff today. Today was Wednesday, and I was almost out of time. I had to ask Bailey about the witness protection program today. I had to ask her why the Salvatores would want her dead. That ought to be a fun conversation.

I walked down the stairs—the living room was empty. I decided to wait for Mike out on the porch. It was even colder today. I rubbed my bare arms as I pulled out my phone and called Emma. She answered on the first ring.

"Are you okay? I've been worried sick about you. I left you a message last night."

"Sorry," I said. "I didn't get the message." Which wasn't a lie. I didn't realize Emma had left a message.

"How is the undercover work going? Did you find the witness?"

"I think so," I said.

"Is she willing to talk to me?"

"I don't know yet. I'm going to ask her later today. Do you think you could come to Galena?" I asked. "If she is willing to talk, we need to get this story out quickly." I was still hoping there was enough time left to tell the story and catch the killers before they disappeared. They would be gone once the book was released tomorrow night.

There was a long pause and then Emma said, "I don't know. I doubt my teacher is going to just let me leave."

"Even for a big story?"

"I'll see what I can do, but I might just have to talk to her on the phone."

I jumped as the door opened behind me.

"There you are, Finbar."

It was Betty. I motioned to her that I'd be with her in a minute, but she kept talking.

"What are you doing out here without a jacket? Come on in and warm up."

"Is that Betty?" Emma asked. "Oh, I love Betty. Put her on so I can say hi."

"Seriously," I replied.

"Yes!" Emma said enthusiastically.

So I handed the phone to Betty. "A mutual friend of ours would like to say hi."

Betty didn't seem worried, confused, or shocked. She grabbed the phone and started talking like it all made perfect sense.

"Hello?" Betty said into the phone.

"Oh yes, dear. Of course I remember you. How wonderful to hear your voice again," Betty said. "Well, how is it that you know Finbar?"

I held my breath as Betty listened to Emma's answer. I hoped she didn't say *Finbar who?*

CHAPTER FORTY-SEVEN

Betty continued to talk to Emma as she walked back into the house. Was I supposed to walk in after her? Was she going to bring my phone back? Or had Emma accidentally told her who I really was? Maybe she was calling her cop client friend right now.

But she came back out several minutes later with my phone in one hand and another necklace in the other. This necklace didn't have a giant eye on it, though. This one looked even worse.

"Oh, I just love that little Emma so much," Betty said. "She has such a wonderful aura. You're lucky to have her as a friend."

Was Emma a friend? I guess she was quickly becoming one. "I agree," I said.

Betty handed me my phone and lifted the necklace high above her head.

"This is a very strong amulet," Betty said. "Very strong magic. It'll help."

She motioned for me to lean over so she could put it on me. It looked like she had sewn some sort of small burlap sack to a piece of rope. I almost vomited at the smell as I leaned forward.

"What's that smell?" I asked as my eyes watered and my nose started to run.

"That's ghost pepper and garlic. Ghost pepper is a million times hotter than cayenne. In India, they use it to ward off evil."

"Evil?" I asked.

"Yes, and elephants. They smear it on fences." She placed it around my neck and tucked it into my shirt on top of the eye amulet. "Just keep it tucked in and you won't even notice it."

I looked down. It looked like I had a small pillow under my shirt now.

"Thank you."

"You're welcome. Just make sure to leave it on, okay?"

"I will."

"What time is your friend coming? Do you want to wait inside?"

I looked down at my phone. It was already quarter to

eight. It looked like Mike wasn't coming. We actually hadn't talked about him picking me up. . . . I guess I just assumed.

"Maybe I was supposed to meet him at his place," I lied again. "I'm going to walk over there. Thanks again for the amulet."

I started up High Street, toward the stairs, but then I remembered Douglas. I couldn't just go walking down the side of the highway. What if he drove by? What if they found his car and the cops were all down on Main Street right now? I decided to try to find a less-traveled route to school.

I took a left at the end of Betty's block and continued to climb the steep streets that zigzagged toward the top of the bluff. I pulled out my phone and mapped a course that kept me off all main roads and highways. It looked to be an hour on foot. I had no problem missing Nonnemacher's class, but I had to hurry if I was going to make it in time for nutrition with Bailey. Somehow I had to ask her about the witness protection. I had to find out who was trying to kill her and why. And I had no idea how I was going to do that. Maybe Emma would make it up here after all. She was a journalist. Maybe she would know how to approach the topic without freaking Bailey out.

CHAPTER FORTY-EIGHT

I *walked for forty-five minutes on dirt country roads* until I finally saw the school. The bell to end first period rang as I opened the door. Good. I couldn't handle seeing Nonnemacher today. I just wanted to get together with Bailey. Maybe I'd even show her the chapters of my dad's new book. If she was the girl in the photo album, Emma could write the story, and maybe we could catch Anton.

Mike wasn't in class when I walked in, so I decided to sit next to Bailey.

"Okay, class. Settle down. Are we ready to begin?" Metzel asked.

"Today you're going to work in your small groups. You will be making some decisions today, right? You will be deciding on your dish—the healthy dish you will share at our potluck tomorrow. And, like we discussed yesterday, it must promote good cholesterol.

"Okay, guys," Metzel continued, "let's break into our small groups and get to work."

Finally! I turned to Bailey.

"So, what are you thinking? Salad?" I asked.

"Salad? We can do better than salad," Susan interjected.

"Okay. What? Like fish?" I was the last guy to comment on healthy eating. And I suddenly remembered I was starving. I hadn't eaten a thing since I'd washed the Snickers bar down with a Coke last night.

"How about something with pork?" Susan said.

"Pork?" I questioned.

"Yeah. My cousins live over in Dubuque. My uncle is a hog farmer and he swears that pork is the healthiest meat you can eat. I guess Iowa raises more pork than anywhere in the world. His farm smells god-awful, but it's really, really healthy, I guess."

"Pork is healthy?" I asked.

"Actually, Susan," Bailey said, "your uncle is right. Pork is low in cholesterol."

"Okay, let's make pork chops," I said.

"My uncle gave me a great pineapple-and-pork recipe." Susan was excited now. "We could make that. It's delicious."

"Okay," Bailey said. "Let's do that. We can meet at my

house right after school. Susan, you bring the pork, and Finbar, you bring the pineapple. I'm sure I'll have everything else."

"We've got a half a hog in the freezer," Susan said. "He's from my uncle's farm. I could bring that."

"Well, that might be a lot," Bailey said. "How about just a couple of pork chops?" Bailey quickly added, "Maybe just from the store?"

"But that won't get us points with Metzel." Susan sounded confused now.

"Sure it will. The recipe came from your uncle, right?"

"Yeah. Do you think that's enough?"

"I think so," Bailey replied.

"I don't know," I said. "I think Susan might be right. We might want that hog from her freezer." I smiled at Bailey.

"Half hog," Susan corrected.

"Right. Half hog." I loved the thought of Susan dragging half a hog into Bailey's house.

"A couple of chops will do," Bailey said quickly.

"What's your address?" I asked.

"Here." Bailey grabbed the pen and notebook from my desk. "I'll draw you a map."

She uncapped my pen and fanned through my notebook. She stopped suddenly.

"What's this?" She was wearing a sly, angled grin as she opened a page.

"What?" I grabbed the corner of the notebook to see what she was looking at. It was the list I had made of girls in Mike's class that might fit the description of the girl in my dad's book. I had starred, circled, and underlined Bailey's name . . . several times.

"Oh, man! It's not what you think," I said.

Her smile widened. "Hey, Finny. I'm not thinking anything."

"Man, it's a five-subject notebook, and you pick that page!" My cheeks were burning.

She didn't respond, drawing a map on the page. She closed the notebook and handed it to me as the bell rang. She stood up, winked, and said, "See you after school, Finny."

I sat and waited until she had left the room. I opened my notebook and flipped through it looking for the page with the map. I found the page. It was covered in ink. Bailey had drawn a detailed map of The Territories. It included her address and a star where her house was located.

CHAPTER FORTY-NINE

Mike hadn't shown up for school today. *And as I* entered the lunchroom, I realized Ben, Scott, and Trish were all gone too. I hoped they were just skipping school or something. I wouldn't forgive myself if Duane and his buddies hurt Mike because of what I did to him. I suddenly wished I had asked Mike for his cell number.

I got into line and ordered two cheeseburgers, fries, tots, and pudding. I looked toward the cheerleaders' table. Bailey was sitting next to Amanda. What the heck, I had nothing to lose. I scanned the football player's table as I headed toward Bailey. Duane wasn't there.

"Do you mind if I join you?"

"Sure." Bailey said as she slid down and made room between her and Amanda.

Amanda made a gagging noise as she motioned to my tray. "Eat much?"

"Well, Bailey here kept talking about pork and hog halves during class. It made me hungry," I said.

"That's disgusting," Amanda said, sounding truly repulsed.

"That's what I told her."

"Oh my god," Bailey said. "I was so sure Susan was going to drag a dead pig into my living room. My dad would freak."

"Hey, she was just supporting her uncle's butchering business," I said with a shrug. Bailey laughed.

"Oh god, speaking of butchering." Bailey suddenly looked ill. "Did you hear about Happy Puppy?"

"No," I said. "I saw it in the paper but didn't read the article."

"Oh my god," Amanda burst out, "I heard about that."

"What?" I asked again.

"The Happy Puppy Dog Food Company. It's just down the highway. Apparently three or four workers fell into, or got sucked into, a meat-processing machine," Bailey said.

"Yeah," Amanda said, "but I heard they weren't all employees. Like one of the employees was showing his family around the place and they fell in, or something."

"How is that even possible?" I asked, fully knowing how

it was possible. Anton or one of the other guys clearly had pushed them in. Or killed them first and ground them into puppy chow to make it look like an accident.

"They've got huge machines over there," Amanda said. "My brother worked there one summer. They just shove entire cow carcasses in—brains and all. They just grind that stuff up and feed it to Fido."

"So, the worst part is—"

I cut Amanda off. "The worst part? Like the family getting ground up isn't bad enough?"

"No, it gets worse. Apparently they didn't realize what had happened right away. Like it took a couple of days before they pieced it together."

"No pun intended," I inserted.

"Right." Bailey laughed. "So some of the dog food shipped out with the Henderson family in it."

"That's why they pulled over the trucks yesterday," I asked.

"Yup. I heard some of it had already hit the shelves in Chicago."

I took a bite of my cheeseburger. "You guys have one weird town. Hay balers and dog-food machines eating people. Not to mention the article I read about a water heater killing a guy."

"Don't forget about Schneider," Bailey said.

"How can I?" Amanda asked. "I was one of the ones who saw him." She shivered. "Gross."

"What did he look like?" Bailey asked.

"Bailey! That's disgusting!"

"What? You brought it up. I'm just saying."

"It's weird," Amanda said. "I mean, it's like they're there, but they're not. You know? He was so still."

My phone started ringing and I tried to fish it out of my pocket. I hoped it was Emma saying she was on her way.

"You can't use your phone in school," Amanda scolded. "They'll take it way."

"I just need to talk for, like, two seconds," I said.

I stood up and turned my back to Amanda and Bailey. I hit the answer button and was raising the phone to my ear when a massive fist smashed into it. My phone shattered on the floor.

"There are no phones in school."

I looked up, half expecting to see Duane. It wasn't Duane. It was one of the other giant football players.

"That was my third phone this week!" I yelled.

"I don't care."

How was I going to pay Betty if I had to keep buying phones? I looked at the pieces on the floor. I could feel a fire starting to burn in my gut. Or maybe it was the ghost pepper amulet.

"You're gonna buy me a new phone," I demanded.

The guy folded his arms. He was a big guy, but nowhere near as big as Duane. He was tucking his hands in behind his biceps, trying to push them up. Trying to look like the big man in front of his buddies. But I could tell, he was scared. He had to be scared of what I did to Duane.

"Did you have a good lunch?" I asked. "'Cause I'm hungry and I'm looking forward to eating those cheeseburgers. So why don't you just give me sixty bucks and we'll pretend this didn't happen."

"Screw you."

"Were you there the other night? With Duane?" I asked. "At the pool?"

"Yeah, I was there. And I know you're a dead man."

"Hey, I'm here. Where's your buddy? Is he still picking his teeth out of the pool?"

"Where are *your* buddies?" he asked.

"What are you talking about?"

"Oh, we found *your* buddies last night at the bowling alley. Maybe they are still there picking *their* teeth out of the gutter."

CHAPTER FIFTY

I **tried to shove the guy backward, but he didn't move**
very far. I could hear several of his buddies getting up from
their table now.

"You better hope my friends are all right," I said, leaning
down toward his face.

"Or what?"

Several of the other football players were standing behind
him now. Arms crossed. *All for one and one for all*, I thought.

I reached down and put one of my tater tots into my
mouth. I was starving, but I was also trying to show the pack
of idiots that I wouldn't scare easily. *Never show them any
fear*, my dad had said.

"I think we all need to talk, don't you?" I asked, poking

him in his thick chest. "I think we should get together after school and settle this thing."

"Fin!" Bailey sounded scared. "Don't be crazy. Plus, you're supposed to be at my place after school."

Great, I thought. Now they'll know exactly where to find me.

"Yeah, with two fresh pineapples," I added. "I'll be there. Why don't you boys meet me over at the Piggly Wiggly after school. I've got to get some pineapples. We can settle this thing and then I'm going to Bailey's."

"You're a dead man, dude," one of the football players said.

"We'll see." I grabbed another tot and walked out of the cafeteria.

I was seriously angry about my phone. I had to go buy another phone, and I was pretty sure I had taken the last of the cheap ones at the Pig. I would be forced to buy the gold standard in mobile phones. It was sure to wipe me out.

I walked down the hall toward my next class. I had three more hours of sitting in classes that meant nothing to me. *Forget it*, I thought. I'd already gotten what I needed. I'd be at Bailey's house in a couple of hours. After Susan left, I'd show her the chapters from my dad's new book and ask her what she knew. Ask her if she would tell her story to Emma and the world. Before it was too late. Before the killers moved on.

I ripped Bailey's map out of my notebook and threw the

rest in the trash. I walked quickly toward the main entrance. It was early October, but it suddenly felt like June. Like the last day of school.

I stopped walking about ten feet from the front door. Nonnemacher had taken my phone. My brand-new phone. I didn't need to buy a new one. I knew exactly where I could find a perfectly good phone. And it was my last day at Galena High. I had nothing to lose.

Nonnemacher was in the middle of some sort of rant in Spanish as I pushed open his classroom door. He stopped immediately.

"*¿Lo que en el mundo se cree que está haciendo, señor Jennings?*"

"I've got no idea what you just said." I walked straight to his desk and opened the middle drawer. Nothing. There were pens and papers, but no phone.

Nonnemacher switched to English.

"What in god's name do you think you're doing?" he demanded.

"Taking my phone back," I said, as I pulled open another drawer. Bingo. I grabbed my piece of crap pay-as-you-go.

"I distinctly remember saying that you would get it back at the end of the school year."

I turned and looked at him. His face was red. His eyes looked like they were rattling in their sockets.

"It *is* the end of the school year for me. *Adiós.*"

CHAPTER FIFTY-ONE

I *walked down the hall and out the front door. I* didn't bother to look back. I knew Nonnemacher wouldn't follow me.

I set out for the Piggly Wiggly. I needed to get the pine-apples and then start walking south to The Territories. There was clearly no way I was waiting around for the football team to beat my head in. I couldn't fight an entire team. No, I'd get the pineapples and get a head start to Bailey's.

There were only two cars in the parking lot when I reached the Pig. Neither of them were Douglas's. Unless he hadn't found his car yet and had rented a new one. This was a bad idea. What if Douglas told the store manager to be on the lookout for me? What if Douglas was around somewhere, staking the place out? I slowed down as I walked toward the automatic door. This couldn't be a good idea. I looked around. No cops. No sign of Douglas. And no WANTED pictures of me taped to the windows. I was going to get the pineapples and get the heck out.

The Pig had a mountain of fresh pineapples. I grabbed two and headed to the checkout. There was a woman standing at the same cash register Trish had been at the night before. The same one I had hidden under. I was definitely pushing my luck. But I paid for the pineapples and got out of the store, no problem.

I crossed the highway and walked about a mile down a dirt road. I wondered if this stupid Podunk town had a bus. But I guessed with only eight hundred residents and miles of farm fields, it wouldn't have made sense. I would have to walk all the way to The Territories. I decided to take back roads. I wasn't taking any chances with Douglas. My phone said it was three hours to The Territories on foot. I needed to be at Bailey's in two and a half. And I certainly needed to get there before the football team figured out I wasn't going to show up at the Pig and they came looking for me. Maybe I could run and even stop by Mike's before Bailey's. I needed to know he was okay.

Despite my best efforts, it took me more than two hours to reach The Territories. But the freaking Territories were huge, and Bailey's map wasn't exactly drawn to scale, so it took me another hour to find Bailey's house.

I shoved Bailey's map into my pocket as I rang the door-bell. I waited a few minutes, but no one answered. I tried again. I was almost an hour late. Were they already done? Had the idiot football guys come out looking for me and caused trouble?

I looked in the front window. It looked dark inside. I pulled the map out and looked at the address again. This was definitely the right house. I sat down on the front step to wait.

I thought about my new phone in a million pieces on the lunchroom floor. I wondered if Emma had left a message on that phone. I pulled my old phone from my pocket and called Emma. She didn't answer. I hung up as a car pulled into the driveway. Bailey and Susan got out. Bailey was hold-ing two pineapples.

"There you are," Bailey said. She had changed clothes since school. She was wearing faded jeans and a tight sweater.

"Hey, sorry I'm late." I held up my two pineapples. "I guess we can make twice as much now."

"I got worried when you didn't show," Bailey said. "I thought something might have gone wrong at the Pig."

"What could have gone wrong?" I asked with a smile.

"Oh, I don't know. Maybe the entire football team using you as a tackling dummy."

CHAPTER FIFTY-TWO

Bailey twisted the handle and pushed the door open.

"You don't lock your doors?" I asked.

"This is Galena. Nothing happens in Galena. It's, like, the safest place on the planet," she said.

"If you say so."

Bailey paused for a moment and then said, "Whoa, what's that smell?"

Oh, no. Betty's amulet. All the sweat from running out here must have aggravated the peppers.

"I don't smell anything," I said. And I wasn't lying. I must have grown used to the stench. All I could smell was Bailey. And she smelled fantastic.

Susan was standing five feet behind us.

"No, I smell it too. It smells like bad chimichanga."

"Bad chimichanga?" I repeated.

"Yeah. Once my uncle made my cousins and I some pork chimichangas and he wanted them to be authentic Mexican chimichangas, so he soaked them in jalapeño oil overnight. Then he burned them. It smells like that."

"Jalapeño oil?" I asked.

"Authentic burned jalapeño oil," Susan replied.

"Whatever," Bailey said as she walked into her house.

"Susan and I already started. The pork chops are cooked, we just need to add the pineapple."

Bailey's living room was a maze of boxes. Some opened. Some taped shut.

"I see you guys still haven't fully unpacked." Which seemed strange. Bailey's family would have been relocated here months ago. That's a long time to live out of boxes.

"Guess again, Finny. We're heading the other direction."

"What? Moving?"

"Bingo," Bailey said as she cut the top off one of the pine-apples. "And my dad has been working so much, he told me to throw all this stuff into boxes. Nice, huh?"

"But didn't you just get here?" I asked.

"Yeah, but my—" Bailey paused. "How did you know we just moved here?"

Shoot. Way to go, Furious.

"I, ah, I asked Mike about you." That was worse. Now I

looked pathetic. First the notebook, and now this pathetic schoolboy thing.

"Oh, really?" She smiled.

"When are you moving?" Susan asked as she stepped into the kitchen to help Bailey cut up the pineapple.

"When aren't we moving? Who knows? Soon, I guess. We're always moving."

I laughed. "I know a little about that."

"Really? Tell us a little about yourself, Finny. Who is Finbar Jennings and what is he all about?" Bailey said as she took a bite of pineapple.

He's a kid I went to school with in Ireland, I thought. *And I actually don't know much about him.*

"Oh, you know. Same old story. I've moved around the world with my mom. A different town and country every few months. New adventures. New friends. New languages. Nothing too exciting." I smiled.

"Right," Bailey said as she bent over to get a cutting board for Susan. "Us too."

I glanced into a couple of the open boxes in front of me. One was full of stuffed animals. I grabbed a monkey.

"Still sleeping with stuffed animals, I see." I held the monkey up by one arm.

"Hey! That's Mr. Ooh Ooh. Be careful with him! Ooh Ooh and I have been through a lot together," Bailey said.

"He's cute," Susan added.

"Thank you."

I put Mr. Ooh Ooh down and played with a couple of the stuffed animals. Anything to keep my distance from Bailey and Susan. I didn't want them to smell the ghost pepper amulet. I realized my eyes and nose were running now.

I saw a photo album in another open box and thumbed through it. There were pictures of a little girl at Disney. The little girl sitting on a pony. The girl in the desert. At the beach. And then a more recent picture of Bailey with a guy, presumably her dad. My brain tingled. Somewhere deep down I had a faint feeling I had seen him before.

"Who's this?" I asked, holding up the photo.

"Oh, that's me and my dad in Millennium Park."

I set the photo album down and picked up another one. I opened it up, and on the first page was a picture of an older woman next to an obituary. The obituary said the woman had been survived in death by sixteen grandchildren. Bailey must have been one of the sixteen grandchildren.

"Bailey?"

"Yeah."

"Do you have a lot of cousins?" I asked.

"We're Catholic and Italian," she said. "What do you think?"

"Yup," I replied. "Lots of cousins. I'm guessing fifteen, give or take."

"I don't know. I've never really counted."

I continued to flip through the book. Every page had a photo on the left and then either an obituary or some newspaper clipping detailing some horrible death on the right. Maybe it was an Italian thing? Heck, my mom always saved those little bookmarks they passed out at funerals.

I kept flipping through Bailey's morbid family tree. And most of the members shared a family resemblance. An old Italian man, a young Italian man, older woman, younger woman, and then . . . and then I felt all the blood rush from my head. There, on the left side of the page, was a picture of my mother. And on the right . . . an article detailing the shooting outside the DeSoto House Hotel.

CHAPTER FIFTY-THREE

I *stared at the page. I hadn't seen her face in months.*

"What are you looking at now?" Bailey asked.

I didn't answer. I read the first few lines of the article. The newspaper clipping gave an account of my mother being gunned down. My knees were shaking as I flipped to the next page. There was another photo and another obituary for a man I didn't recognize. The obituary said he had died in a fire. I flipped to the next. There was a picture of an older woman. Maybe late forties or early fifties. But the right side of the page was empty. No newspaper clipping. No obituary. I flipped to the next.

"Oh my god!"

"What? What is it, Finny? Did you find one of my old report cards?" Bailey asked.

It was Trish. She was a little younger in the photo, but it was Trish. The woman and Trish had no obituaries. No proof of death. *Because they're still alive*, I thought. It was just like in my dad's book. This must have been the Sicilian's book of proof.

"Where did you get this?" I asked, holding up the book.

"I don't recognize that one. It must be my dad's."

Her dad? How did he—

Bailey's dad had to be Anton. It was the only thing that made sense. Bailey said they had moved from city to city, just like my mom and me. They hadn't been in Galena too long and now they were moving. Right before my dad's book came out, naming him as the killer. And how else would he have this book? Bailey's dad was working late all right: He was killing Trish and the other woman before they left Galena. He was finishing up the Sicilian's work.

I tucked the photo album into the back of my pants. I tried to talk, but my voice cracked.

"Bailey—" I stopped, cleared my throat, and tried again. "Bailey, what does your dad do?"

"I don't really know," she answered. "He's, like, some sort of accountant or something. He's a contractor for the government or army or something."

"That's weird," I mumbled.

"Why is that weird?" Bailey asked.

"'Cause that's what my mom did too."

I started toward the door. Bailey's family wasn't in the witness protection program. Her dad was killing the people in the witness protection program.

"Where are you going?"

"I need to check on Mike. Do you know where he lives?" I asked.

"Yeah, he and Trish live down the street by the golf course. But don't you want to finish cooking?"

I didn't answer Bailey. I just started running down the driveway.

How had I screwed up so badly?

I turned the corner and could see the golf course. Mike's house was just over the hill. I ran for twenty minutes and then slowed to a walk and tried to catch my breath. The amulet was now blistering my chest.

I walked down the middle of the road for three or four minutes until I saw the gate to Mike's house. I figured I would show Mike and Trish the photo album and tell them they were in danger, if I wasn't too late.

I was about to walk down their driveway when I noticed a dark-blue sedan parked several hundred feet past the drive. The sedan kind of looked like—

I started to run, but it was too late. Douglas was already out of the car and running after me. I turned to run faster, but my legs were numb and my knees were buckling from running all afternoon. I heard Douglas yell my name as I crossed the street and headed for the golf course. There was no way I could outrun him this time. I made it about ten more feet before Douglas jumped on my back and I dropped the photo album as we collapsed to the ground.

He flipped me over and grabbed my arms. He was strong. And angry. His eyes were crazed. He looked like he wanted to kill me. He placed his knee over my right bicep and applied a ton of pressure. It hurt like crazy. It felt like he was pushing my muscle clean off the bone. I tried to free my arm, but it was pointless. With both of his hands free, he made a move toward my left arm. I pulled it in close to my chest. Then, without thinking, I thrust my palm up and out as hard as I could. The base of my palm smashed into Douglas's nose. I could feel the cartilage give as my hand pushed his nose up and into his skull.

Douglas grabbed his face with both hands.

"God, what are you doing, Furious? Are you crazy?" Douglas yelled through his cupped hands.

Blood was gushing from his nose. I tried to pull my right hand free but couldn't. Douglas's body was up off my chest and now he was kneeling on my right bicep with all of his weight. Crushing it.

"Get off me!" I pulled back my left hand and hit him as hard as I could in the chest. Nothing. I wiped Douglas's blood from my face and hit him again. But this time I aimed for the groin. I used every ounce of energy I had left. I punched as hard as I could. I tried to punch through him. It worked. Douglas shifted his weight as he moved his concern from his face to his crotch. I pushed him to the side and got to my feet. I was about five feet away when he tackled me again.

"You're not getting away this time," he said as he jerked my right arm out from under me. He placed his knee in the small of my back and yanked my left arm out from under me too.

"You busted my nose!" He sounded shocked.

I could hear the clank of metal as he slapped the hand-cuffs on me. This was it. I was going to die.

CHAPTER FIFTY-FOUR

I **stayed** **facedown** **for** **what** **felt** **like** **forever** **before**
Douglas picked me up off the ground. He looked bad.

"Walk," he grunted as he reached down and picked up
the photo album.

I walked toward Mike and Trish's house.

"The car!" Douglas yelled. "Walk to the car."

Was he going to lock me in the car while he went in to
kill Trish? Could I run? Could I turn around and kick Douglas and run?

Douglas opened the passenger door and shoved me in.
I landed face-first on the seat. I tried to sit up before he got
around to the driver's side, but I couldn't sit on the car's seat
with my hands cuffed behind my back. I bounced to the edge

of the seat and tried to lean back on my shoulders. It hurt, but not as badly as Douglas had to be hurting.

Douglas got in, threw the photo album in the backseat, and started the car. He adjusted the rearview mirror to get a better look at his face.

"You broke it in two places, for crying out loud." He slammed the car into drive and pulled away.

Two places? I don't know what Douglas saw, but it looked to be broken in at least six places and blood was flowing down his face.

I stared out the window as we drove toward town. We turned onto Main Street and drove past the floodgates. It was dinnertime, and downtown was full of tourists. I thought about yelling for help. Or smashing my head against the window to get someone's attention. But I was a kid in handcuffs and Douglas was an agent with a gun and a badge. I lose.

We drove to the end of Main Street and stopped in front of a small brick building with bars on the windows and flower boxes beneath them. The sign above the door read Galena Police Department. It was just like my dad had described it in his book.

Douglas pulled me out of the car and dragged me through the front door. Inside, there was a low counter with a heavy man sitting behind it. He was reading the *Galena Gazette*.

"Can I help you?" he asked without looking up.

"Yeah, I'm Director Douglas with the CIA."

The cop looked up. He had a round face and a bushy gray mustache. I had seen him before. He was the cop that had gotten a palm reading at Betty's.

"The what?" He set the paper on his lap.

"The CIA," Douglas said. "The Central Intelligence Agency."

"I know what the CIA is. Wow, man, you look like hell."

"Thanks. Look"—Douglas took his badge out of his pocket and showed it to the cop—"I need a favor. I need you to watch this kid while I go get my nose looked at."

"Did he do that?" The cop motioned to Douglas's face.

"No. I fell."

"Right. Is the boy under arrest?"

"Not yet. I just need you to detain him. Where can I find a doctor in this town?" Douglas asked.

"For something like that"—the cop motioned to Douglas's face again—"you've got to go to Dubuque. They've got three hospitals over there."

"How far is Dubuque?"

"Oh, I'd say twenty to twenty-five minutes, depending."

"And you'll watch the kid?"

"Sure," the cop said.

"Thanks. I'll be back as soon as possible." Douglas left a trail of blood behind him as he walked out the door.

"You sure did a number on him," the cop said.

"He fell," I said.

"Sure he did. Come on and have a seat." The cop motioned for me to walk around and sit at the desk behind him.

I tried to sit but couldn't get comfortable with my hands behind my back.

"Oh, shoot." The cop stood up. "Here, let me see that." He motioned for me to turn around. "If you ain't under arrest, why have the cuffs on you, right?"

He removed the handcuffs and my arms fell to my sides.

"Thank you." I tried to raise my arms in front of me but couldn't.

"Don't worry about that. You'll feel good as new in a few minutes. Takes a while for the blood to start flowing."

The cop went back to reading the paper, and my phone rang several minutes later.

"Do you mind if I get that?" I asked.

"Suit yourself."

I pulled out my old phone. It was Emma.

"Hey, what's up?"

"Hey, Furious. You sound kind of funny. Why are you talking so softly?"

"Yeah, it is a nice day," I replied.

"What?"

"No, I haven't had a chance to do that yet. I've been sort of tied up," I said.

"What are you talking about? Are you okay?" Emma asked.

"No," I said.

"Are you in trouble?"

"Yup."

"Can I help?"

"That would be great."

"What's wrong? Where are you?"

I thought for a minute and then said, "Same place your dad went."

"Jail? You're in jail?"

"That's right."

"In Galena?"

"The one and only."

"Sit tight. I'm on my way."

"I'll try," I said as I pushed the cancel button.

I sat staring at the walls for the next hour, wondering if I could trust the sheriff. Could I tell him that Bailey's dad was a CIA-trained assassin? And that her dad had secretly been working with the Salvatore crime syndicate and was probably responsible for my mom's murder and, at this very minute, was on his way to kill Trish and the woman in the photo—

The photo album! Douglas had taken the photo album.

The only physical proof I had to connect my dad's book to Anton and the others. And he never asked about it. Douglas just picked it up like he knew what it was.

The front door opened suddenly, and I practically jumped out of my seat. I figured it was Douglas, back to take me somewhere private. But I looked up and saw Betty.

CHAPTER FIFTY-FIVE

*H*ello, Maynard," she said, without looking at me.

"Betty? What are you doing here?" The cop set the newspaper on the desk in front of him.

"I have a favor to ask," Betty said as she stepped up to the counter.

"What is it?"

"Well, Finbar there is my nephew, and I heard he was in a bit of trouble." Betty motioned to me.

The cop looked back at me. "He's your nephew? Gosh, Betty, I thought I recognized him from the other day."

"Yes. Have you arrested him, Maynard?" she asked.

"Well, no, Betty. I'm just watching him for, uh . . . ah—"

"Is he under arrest?" Betty asked.

"No."

"Well, then, can I take him home?"

The cop looked at me and then back at Betty. "Well geez, Betty. You know I'd love to help you out, but I'm not sure I should—"

Betty cut him off. "What has he done?" Betty demanded.

"Well." The cop looked at me. "I guess I'm not sure. Come to think of it, the agent didn't really say."

"Well, Maynard, can you really hold someone without a reason? Especially when that someone is my nephew?"

The cop looked at her without answering.

"I'm going to take him home and you can just tell this agent fellow where he is, okay?"

The cop paused for a moment and then said, "Well, I don't see why not. I mean, since he's your nephew, and all." He paused. "Sure, go on and take him home. I'll just let the federal guy know where to find him."

I stood up.

"Well, I appreciate that, Maynard. I hope he hasn't caused you too much trouble." Betty motioned to me.

"No. No. No trouble at all."

I thought I saw a smile under the cop's massive mustache.

"No trouble at all," he said again.

I didn't say a word. I just walked around the counter.

"Thank you, Maynard," Betty said. "I'll see you on Tuesday."

"Yes, I'll see you Tuesday at the regular time."

CHAPTER FIFTY-SIX

I *didn't say a word as we stepped out onto Main Street.*

"I prefer the name Furious to Finbar," Betty said.

"Yeah, me too. How did you find out?" I asked.

"I got a call from that nice Emma girl. She asked me to help you out. She said you'd been through a lot lately. But that much I already knew. Your colors were so dark. She's on her way up here, but I figured Maynard would listen to me. He's a little sweet on me."

"Yes, I see that. But I'm sorry you got involved," I said. "Now this federal guy is going to come by your place looking for me. I'm afraid he's not such a nice guy."

"Oh, don't you worry about me. I'm just thankful I know

the truth. I thought I was losing my mind when your charts weren't adding up."

"Yeah." I looked down. "I felt bad about that too. And you were right, by the way: I am a Taurus."

Betty clapped her hands together. "Ha! I knew it!"

"Thank you for getting me out, but I've got to go help a friend."

"What's wrong? Is there something I can do to help? Maybe we could get Maynard to help. He really is a sweet man."

"I appreciate the offer, but I need to do this on my own. You don't happen to have a car, do you?"

"Sorry, hon, I don't drive."

"That's okay," I started walking down Main Street. "Please be careful if Douglas comes to see you."

Betty called out, "Don't worry. If he tries anything funny, I'll put a curse on him that will make him wish he'd never met me. And I ain't bluffin'!"

I ran down Main Street, past the floodgates, to the highway. I set out at a good pace, but it was going to take more than two hours to get to The Territories. I decided that I'd buy a motorcycle when I got back to . . . wherever it was I would live when this was done. No more running. I hated running.

I ran for thirty minutes before slowing to a walk. I was too slow. And The Territories were too far. Bailey's dad, Anton, had probably already gotten to Trish. I pulled out my phone to call information. Maybe they had a home line that was listed and I could call and warn them, but my phone just beeped. No signal.

I started to run again when I heard the roar of a semi truck coming over the hill in front of me. I ran for about twenty feet before I stopped. I could see the truck now and it had seen me. It wasn't a semi truck, it was a bright orange pickup, and it was crossing the highway and coming toward me. I jumped over the metal guardrail, and the truck stopped in front of me. Four huge guys jumped out of the bed of the truck, and Duane and another guy climbed out of the cab. Man, this was the last thing I needed. I stepped back onto the highway.

"Well, well, well. Looky here, boys, we've got ourselves a hitchhiker," Duane said.

Duane's face was covered with bandages, but I could see a little black-and-blue skin peeking out from the edges. The six guys stood shoulder to shoulder on the side of the road.

"Look, guys, I'm not looking for trouble, here." I slipped my phone into my pocket.

"Do you need a lift, Finbar?"

"No, thanks," I said.

Their bodies had formed a giant roadblock. There was no way I was going to get past them.

"You broke my buddy's nose," one of them said.

"Yeah, I see that. And I hear you hurt my friends," I said.

"Oh, we did. And we're going to hurt you," he replied.

"I'm going to break your nose and your legs," Duane added.

And I believed them.

"Well, you're going to try," I said.

They all laughed.

"And you might succeed. Heck, you might even kill me. But I promise at least three or four of you will have season-ending injuries when we're done here."

"You're insane."

"Count on it," I said.

"Hey, why don't you show these guys your little necklace." Duane laughed.

"Yeah, I want to see this thing," one of them shouted.

"What a great idea," I said, pulling the giant blue eye out from under my shirt.

"Dude, Duane, you weren't kidding!"

I took off the eye and threw it at their feet.

"You can have it," I said.

"Seriously? Sweet." The guy on the end picked it up. The other five football players stared at him.

"What? It's kind of cool."

"If you think that's cool, wait till you see my new one." I pulled on the rope and fished out the giant pouch of ghost pepper.

"Whoa, look at that thing!" They were howling now. "You're crazy, dude."

I grabbed the pouch and pulled it over my head. I loosened the top of the pouch and flipped it upside down. The oil from the ghost peppers burned my skin as I poured the contents of the pouch into my hand.

"I told you, you can count on it. You can keep the eye, and this one too!"

I ran toward the mass of bodies as fast as I could, closed my eyes, held my breath, and threw the ghost peppers hard. My eyes were burning as I took several steps back. With my eyes still closed, I took off my shirt with my left hand and placed it over my face. Within seconds, I could hear screaming and vomiting, but I still couldn't see. I wiped my eyes with my shirt again and I felt hot blisters forming on my right hand. Betty was playing with some crazy stuff. I no longer worried about Douglas paying her a visit.

I managed to get my left eye open. All six of them were on the ground, writhing in pain. I walked past them, jumped into Duane's truck, closed the door, and put it in drive.

CHAPTER FIFTY-SEVEN

*T*hanks to Duane lending me his truck, I got to The Territories in fifteen minutes. It was another few minutes to Mike and Trish's place. The gate was still open, and I pulled into the drive. Duane's exhaust thundered and crackled as I parked behind Trish's car. There was no sign of Douglas or Bailey's dad. But if they were in there, they certainly knew I was here too. Susan was right: There was nothing subtle about Duane or his truck.

Mike was out of the house before I was out of the truck. Both of his eyes were black and blue, and his lip was split open.

"What are you doing with Duane's truck?" he said with a bit of a lisp.

"Oh, man," I said, getting out of the truck. "Look at what they did to you. I'm so sorry, Mike."

"I told you they would get revenge," Mike said. "I told you."

"I'm sorry, Mike. I should have been there."

"Where were you? You never showed." Mike's lisp was bad. It was hard to understand him.

"Long story," I said. "Is Trish here?"

"She's inside. What's going on with Duane's truck?"

I didn't answer Mike and just headed toward the front door. "Is there anyone else in there?"

"Dude, what do you mean? What's going on, Finbar?"

"Furious," I said. "My name is actually Furious Jones."

Mike stood still. He looked confused.

I put my hands on his shoulders and said, "Look, there is someone coming here to kill Trish. We need to get her out of here right now. We're all in danger."

"Trish is in danger? What are you talking about?"

"Mike, just take me to her. Please."

Mike pushed open the door and I followed him down a hallway to a closed door. He knocked, but I pushed it open before Trish could answer.

Trish was lying on her bed with headphones on, reading a book. She looked up at me. "Hey, Fin, what's going on? Did you see what those guys did to my brother's face?"

"Fin here just drove up in Duane's truck," Mike

blurted out. "Fin here says his name isn't really Finbar."

"What?" Trish looked nervous. She pulled her legs up to her chest. "What's he talking about, Fin?"

"You're in serious trouble, Trish. I know you're in the witness protection program, and I have reason to believe there is a very bad guy on his way right now and he wants you dead."

Trish pushed the hair out of her eyes. Her skin looked milky white against her auburn hair.

"How do you know about that?" she asked. Her voice was soft now. "Did you tell him?" She looked at Mike. She sounded scared. I couldn't imagine what must have happened to make Trish sound so scared.

Mike looked at Trish. "Come on. You know I didn't."

"Who are you? Are you with them? How do you know?" Trish suddenly looked nothing like the girl I had met at the Pig. She was weak. Cowering.

"I'm here to help you. He's coming right now, Trish. We need to get out of here."

"Who's coming?" She started to cry. "What's going on?"

I bent down on one knee.

"My name is Furious Jones. My dad is—" I paused. "My mom was with the CIA. And she was killed in Galena a while back. The guy who killed her is coming here to kill you."

Trish didn't look up. I pushed the hair out of her eyes. "I saw your picture in a photo album of witnesses. There were a bunch of people in the album. There are only two of them still alive, and yours is one of the last pictures. The Salvatores are killing the witnesses, Trish. They want to silence you."

"What do you mean?" she asked.

"Whatever you witnessed. They want to silence you."

Trish looked up at Mike and then back at me.

"I didn't witness anything. I'm not in the program because of what I saw." She paused. "It's what I did."

"What did you do?"

She started to answer when Mike interrupted.

"Trish! No. We don't even know who this guy is!"

"I killed a guy," she said. "A very bad guy."

"Who?" I asked.

She looked up at me, her eyes wide and watery. "My dad."

Trish continued. "Our dad was a bad, bad dude. He had worked for the mob my entire life. Collecting money. Breaking bones. That kind of stuff. One night he brought the violence home." She started crying again. "I had to save my mom."

"Whoa."

"My mom went to the police and told them she would testify against him, and the Salvatore family, if they could protect me." She wiped her nose on her sleeve. "That's how we ended up here. In this stupid little town."

"Oh, man!" I suddenly remembered the other woman in the photo album. "Your mom! Do you have a picture of her?"

I stood up. "There was one other woman in the photo album. Her picture was right before yours."

Mike ran to the living room and grabbed a picture of Trish and a woman sitting on a dock.

"Here," he said. "This is our mom."

I looked at the photo and my heart sank. "That's her," I said. "That was the other woman in the book."

"Are you sure?" Mike asked.

"I don't forget much," I said. "Where is she now?"

"At work."

"Call her right now. Tell her to leave wherever she is and meet us behind the Piggly Wiggly."

Mike didn't move.

"I'm not messing around, Mike." I helped Trish to her feet. "Grab your phone and call her from the truck. We've got to get out of here now in case Anton is coming here to kill Trish first."

"Who's Anton?" Mike asked.

"Bailey's dad," I said. "He's a former CIA assassin who now works for the Salvatores."

CHAPTER FIFTY-EIGHT

*T*he three of us jumped into Duane's truck and headed toward town while Mike tried to reach his mom.

"She's not answering!" he yelled.

"Try her at work," Trish said.

"I did. I called her cell and her work. No one is answering."

"Where does your mom work?"

"Cannova's on Main," Trish said.

Of course she does, I thought. *I should have guessed.*

"It's almost dinnertime," Mike said. "How can no one be answering at the restaurant?"

I stepped down harder on the gas. The truck sprung forward and let out a roar.

"Why do you have Duane's truck?" Trish asked.

"I was walking out here to warn you guys when Duane and his buddies pulled up."

"Duane *and* his buddies?" Mike repeated. "Geez, Finbar, don't tell me you broke their noses too."

"It's Furious. Remember? Furious Jones. And no, I didn't break their noses. Let's just say my good-luck amulet ended up actually being good luck."

"That ugly eye thing?"

"No. A different one. I think the eye was *un*lucky."

"I think you're right," Mike agreed.

"Who are you really?" Trish asked. "And how did you get mixed up in all of this?"

"I know it sounds crazy, but I recently found out my mom worked for the CIA. And the CIA found out about all the Illinois state witnesses being placed in Galena. They sent an assassin to Galena to investigate. Well, it turns out he was working for the Salvatores."

"And that was Bailey's dad?"

"Yup," I said. "Instead of helping, he started killing the witnesses in town. And he made them all look like accidents."

"God, of course. The hay baler, the family at the bait store, that guy with the milking machine, all of those were murders," Trish said.

"I hadn't heard about all of those, but yeah," I said. "That's the kind of stuff he was doing."

"How do you know all of this?" Mike asked.

"Well, the CIA sent my mom here after Anton, Bailey's dad, wasn't stopping the murders. She figured out that Anton was working for the Salvatores—so he killed her."

"How do you know all of this?" Trish asked.

"Well, my dad used to be an investigative reporter, and he came to Galena after my mom's death and investigated."

"Where is your dad now?" Trish asked.

"He's dead," I said. "The Salvatores killed him, too. But not before he wrote everything down. He—"

"Look!" Trish interrupted, pointing up the road. "That's Duane and his buddies."

"It looks like they're up and moving again," I said.

"That's too bad," Mike said.

Duane must have recognized the roar of his truck, because he and his buddies were all moving to the middle of the highway.

"Are they really going to play chicken against a two-ton truck?" I stepped on the gas and brought the truck up to sixty-five miles an hour. The increased roar frightened two of the guys, but the other four stood fast. We were about three-quarters of a mile and closing fast.

"This guy is crazy."

Another one of Duane's buddies bailed. The three smart ones were standing on the right side of the road. I figured I could swerve to the left and miss the guys in the street.

I stepped on the gas a little more, and the last two guys called it quits. Now it was just Duane versus Duane's truck.

"Slow down, Fin—or Furious. He's crazy. He's not going to move," Mike said.

I took my foot off the pedal a bit.

"He'll move," I said. But we were closing fast and Duane wasn't flinching. Was he blind? Could he see us? Had the ghost pepper permanently blinded him? I took my foot completely off the gas and began to coast. The roar of the truck let up a little. We were now two hundred feet from crushing Duane but still had plenty of room to move off to the shoulder and cruise right past him.

Just as I was about to turn the wheel, my head was slammed against the cab wall.

"Screw that!" Trish yelled as she stomped on the gas pedal. Duane never did flinch, but I managed to swerve and miss him by a couple of inches.

"My god, Trish, you could have killed him!"

"We weren't going to kill him," Trish said, "but I'm tired of bullies like Duane ruining my life."

CHAPTER FIFTY-NINE

I *parked the truck in front of Cannova's.*

"That's weird," Mike said. "The CLOSED sign is in the window."

We climbed out of the truck and looked in the window. The restaurant was empty. I wiggled the door handle. The front door was locked.

"The alley," Mike said. "There's a door off the alley."

We ran around the block and found the door. I motioned to Mike and Trish to be quiet as I opened it. The kitchen looked empty. We stepped inside.

"Where's my mom?" Mike cried. "She's not here."

I stepped quietly into the restaurant dining room.

Nothing. I opened the door and looked down the street.

"I think that's Douglas's car down there."

"Who's Douglas?" Trish asked.

"My mom's old boss," I said.

"At the CIA?"

"Yeah. I saw him in town earlier this week. I think he's working with the Salvatores too."

Mike checked the bathrooms and I checked behind the bar. No sign of Anton, Trish's mom, or Douglas.

"What now?" Trish asked. "Where is she?"

"Sheriff Daniels," Mike said. "We have to tell Daniels."

"Yeah," I agreed. We had no other choice. "Let's walk down the alley." I didn't need another run-in with Douglas.

We all walked back into the kitchen and headed for the door when a sound came from behind us. I turned around to see a man closing the door to the walk-in freezer. Our eyes locked. No one said a word. I recognized him from the picture. It was Bailey's dad.

"Hello," he said.

"Where's my mom?" Trish demanded.

"I'm afraid I don't know what you're—"

Trish started to cross the room and the man pulled a gun out of his waistband.

"Now, now, missy. Let's just calm down."

"Where is she?" Trish demanded again.

"Oh, she's close. You'll see her soon enough." The guy cleared his throat. "I'm actually glad you're all here. It saves me a lot of running around."

"Sheriff Daniels is on his way," I lied. "He's got Bailey. He knows all about you, Anton."

The guy stared at me. I felt like I was going cry. He looked cold. Brutal.

"You're not a very good liar, Furious. Your mother would be so disappointed. But maybe you take after your dad. He also had a hard time making things up and felt the need to steal other people's stories."

I felt my chest expanding and could hear the blood pumping hard through my ears. My face was burning. I could tell he was dead set on killing us all.

"Did you kill my mom?"

Anton chuckled a little and started to speak when a small explosion cut him off. Trish had thrown a metal pan at him. It smashed into the metal freezer door just above his head.

He had deflected the pan with his left arm and raised the gun with his right. "You just made my job easier. I don't normally enjoy killing young people, but now . . ." He walked to the oven and turned on a large exhaust fan. It rattled and shook to life. "Muffles the gunfire," he said. "And the screaming."

"There are a ton of people out there on the street. They'll hear you. Please don't," Mike begged.

"Really? They didn't hear your mo—"

Trish was halfway across the room before he could finish the word "mom." I heard another scream and then a gunshot. Trish's body hit the floor. She was five feet in front of me. I could see blood pooling around her as I raced to her side.

Anton pointed the gun at me.

"Back!"

I put my hands up in the air but stayed by Trish's side.

Mike fell to the floor crying.

"Shut up, kid." He pointed the gun at Mike.

Bang!

Bang!

Two more explosions. These were louder than the last. The sound echoed off the ceramic walls and floor. I leaned over to cover Trish's body. My ears were ringing. Mike was screaming, and Anton fell to the floor in front of me.

"What the—"

I was yelling, but I couldn't hear my own voice. I looked up. It was Douglas. His face was now bandaged. He looked just like Duane. And he was pointing his gun at me now.

"Don't move," he commanded.

I looked down at Trish. She had been shot in the shoulder. She was bleeding badly.

"Are you okay?" I asked.

Her lips moved, but I couldn't hear her response. My ears were still ringing. Mike was yelling. Blood was pumping.

"Back up, Furious," Douglas yelled as he pushed Mike toward me.

I covered my ears. God, it hurt. I stood up and walked backward. Mike was yelling something that I couldn't make out.

"What? My ears." I covered my ears again. "I can't hear."

Douglas kept his gun pointed at me as he walked toward Anton.

He was yelling now. "I told you to back up. Now!"

I put my hands in the air and continued to back up.

"Against the counter. Both of you." Douglas motioned for Mike and me to take several more steps backward while he leaned over Anton and checked for signs of life. I backed up until I hit the counter.

Douglas was opening his mouth to say something and then turned toward the door when three more shots rang out. These were muffled. Soft deep thuds. I watched as three bullets ripped through Douglas's soft down vest. Small feathers flew from the holes as Douglas collapsed on top of Anton.

CHAPTER SIXTY

Attorney General Como's athletic body filled the doorway to the dining room. I swore he was wearing the same effortless politician's smile he had worn the night I'd met him at my dad's lecture.

"Hi, Furious," Como said, holding a handgun with a long silencer on the end. "I got your message. I'm glad you reached out to me."

"I'm glad you showed," I said as I lowered my arms. "How did you find me here?"

"Well, I've got a friend or two at the CIA. They told me how to find Douglas and, given Douglas's concern with your family, I figured Douglas would find you. And I was right."

"You knew Douglas was working for the mob?" I asked.

"The mob?" Como asked, sounding offended. "No one uses that term anymore. Mobsters are uneducated, unorganized street punks. The syndicate is a multinational concern with great wealth and power."

"The Salvatore syndicate. You knew he was working for the Salvatores and you didn't stop him?"

"Douglas working for the syndicate?" Como laughed. "Don't be silly. What would they want with him? He's a Boy Scout, for crying out loud. A real pain in the rear."

"I don't understand," I said, looking at Trish bleeding.

"Obviously," Como said, pointing his gun at me. "You don't get to where I am in life, Furious, without having the right friends. The proper connections."

"The Salvatores? *You're* working for the Salvatores?"

He raised his gun and was now pointing it at my head. "I don't work for anyone, son. I'm about to become the president of the United States. But you don't get there without a little help. The Salvatores take care of my problems and, in exchange, I provide them with information."

"Like where the government places its witnesses?" I asked.

"Yeah, stuff like that." He smiled. "It's just business, Furious. And"—he motioned toward Anton's body on the floor—"with Douglas out of the picture, life just got a lot easier for me and the Salvatores. But they aren't going to be happy about Anton. He was a rock star. I mean, he killed your mom. He killed the famous Carson Kidd. Do you know how difficult that was?"

I took a step toward him, and he pulled the trigger. The gun flashed and a bullet whizzed by my head.

"Whoa, I'm a little rusty." He smiled. "Admittedly it has been a long time since I had to hold a gun, but killing is a little like riding a bike—it'll come back to me." He paused and then started to pace in front of the oven.

"It's a shame, really. I mean, I don't enjoy this kind of stuff. Not really. Not like these kinds of guys." He motioned again to Anton's body on the floor. "This is your dad's fault. I mean your mom was just doing her job, I can't blame her for that, but your dad had options."

"I thought you said you were friends with my dad."

"Friends?" He laughed. "In my line of work you don't need friends, you need leverage. And when you showed up at your dad's reading, I thought I finally had it. Did you see his face when he walked onstage and saw us sitting together? I thought for sure he would realize that I meant it when I said I'd kill you if he published the book. With you at my side, I thought for sure he would call off the whole thing. Retract the book and tell everyone to go home. And I think he came close. He paused several times. I mean, did you see how upset he was?" Como laughed.

"In my line of work you end up with a lot of powerful friends and powerful enemies." Then he chuckled again and added, "And sometimes it is hard to tell the difference."

I thought about that night. The last night of my dad's life. He was so upset to see me. Or, at least, I'd *thought* he was upset to see me. I'd thought he didn't want me there. I'd thought it was just one more example of me disappointing him.

"You?" I felt my chest tighten again. "You had my dad killed? And my grandpa?"

"Oh, you're giving me too much credit. I don't have *that* kind of power. The Salvatores had your parents killed. I couldn't help your mom. She dug her own grave when she discovered what was going on here. But your dad. Your dad was all about avenging your mom's death. All about using his popularity to—"

He paused and then smiled. "It's kind of ironic, really. I mean, your dad makes a career out of exploiting your mom, and then, in the end, tries to exploit her for good. Is that irony? I don't know, but I think that's irony."

"You're not going to get away with it," I said.

Como laughed again. "God, you've got so much of your mom—"

Trish let out a weak cough and Como stopped mid-sentence. He looked down at Trish and then at Anton and Douglas.

"Where is your mom?" Como asked Trish. He sounded like he was talking to an infant. I looked back at the counter for something I could use as a weapon as Como repeated the question to Trish.

Trish didn't reply. I wasn't sure she was conscious.

Como pointed the pistol at her and repeated the question again.

"Where is your mom?" he asked. "They're going to want to know the job is done."

"Leave her alone!" Mike roared.

Como smiled. "You must be big brother."

Mike started to cry. "Leave us alone! Please!"

Then Como casually pointed his gun at Mike and fired. He didn't miss this time, and I watched as a bullet entered Mike's foot. The momentum flung him around and he fell to the ground.

"Stop!" I yelled.

He looked back at me. "Oh, we'll get to you soon enough."

"We told the sheriff," I lied again. "He's on his way."

"Please. Are you serious, Furious?" He laughed. "Ha, that rhymed." He continued to smile. "I'm not worried about a small-town sheriff."

He pointed the gun back at me, and I figured this was it. I was sure he would pull the trigger. The guy was absolutely delusional. Everything in my life was gone. He had ripped everything away and now he would end it all.

"I think he already killed her," I said. "Trish's mom. I think Anton killed her and put her in the freezer." I motioned to the freezer door behind him. I had to buy time. "He was walking out of there when we came in."

He turned toward the freezer door and lowered his gun. "He was coming out of here?"

"Yes." You stupid jerk.

"Strange."

He kept the gun pointed in my direction as he backed up. Mike looked at me through his tears and cried harder.

Como switched the gun from his right hand to his left and reached for the freezer door. I looked over my left shoulder. There were a colander and a whisk on the counter.

Como glanced back at us as he pulled the freezer door open. He turned his head to look in. I glanced over my right shoulder. There was nothing on the counter to my right.

Como turned his body and took a half step into the freezer, and I turned around, scouring the shelves behind me. I found a large heavy butcher knife on the top shelf. I gripped it by the tip and spun back around. Como was still standing half in the freezer. His voice was muffled.

"Man, that guy was twisted."

I bent down on one knee and extended my right arm behind me. The knife was heavy.

Concentrate. You've got one chance, I thought.

"Wow," Como continued. "You see? This is why he is— or was—a professional." His voice was becoming louder and clearer as he backed out of the freezer. "That's how professional assassins work. It never looks like murder when done right."

I snapped my arm forward with all my might as Como turned back toward me. I watched the knife flip end over end through the air. It took an eternity to reach his throat. And then Como let out a small scream as the handle of the knife hit him square in the throat and fell to the floor. I guess I didn't have Carson Kidd's, or my mom's, killing talents.

"You little jerk!" He switched the gun back to his right hand and pointed it directly at me. "Do you know who I am? Do you?" he demanded. "Turn around and get on your knees."

He waved the gun back and forth, motioning for me to turn around. "Turn around and get down on your knees!"

This was it. What was I thinking, throwing a butcher knife like I was some sort of fictional hero? I was no hero.

"On your knees now, Furious!"

I turned around and got on my knees. It was going to end—just like this? No fight? No avenging my mom, my dad, or grandpa? Just me living a pathetic life and then kneeling down to die? In the end, my dad tried to avenge my mom's death. But not me. I was just going to kneel down and die.

I could hear his shoes click against the floor as he walked slowly toward me.

"I'll show you how we used to do things." His voice was high now. He was excited.

Several more clicks and I knew he was standing directly behind me. I had to do something. *Fight, Furious! Be strong! Be brave! Like your mom and dad!*

I tightened my stomach and prepared to swing and kick and punch and . . . whatever. I prepared to do something. But as I began to move, I heard a crunch. Had the gun misfired? I tucked down and spun around. I punched with all of my might. I figured I'd punch him like I had punched Douglas. But Como had already fallen, and I hit him in the face. It hurt badly. My hand was bleeding. Como was on his knees with a knife blade sticking out the front of his neck.

Trish pulled the knife out of his throat, and he dropped to the floor.

"Oh my god, Finbar, are you okay?"

I looked down at my hand. There was blood everywhere. "Furious," I said. "My name is Furious."

"Furious."

"I'm okay, are *you*?" I asked.

"I've been worse," she said.

Mike got up and limped to the freezer.

He let out a loud cry and disappeared into it.

"What is it? Is it mom?" Trish cried. I helped Trish to her feet, and we walked to the open door. Their mom was buried under an avalanche of food. She was unconscious and her skin was snow white. But she was still alive. She was taking shallow breaths.

"Accident," I said out loud.

"Accident? This is no accident." Trish turned toward me.

"No. He made it *look* like an accident. Just like the others."

I pulled out my phone and dialed 911.

CHAPTER SIXTY-ONE

I **stood outside and waited for help. Three ambulances** arrived several minutes later. And then the entire Galena Fire Department and police department followed with all their sirens blaring. And then I saw Emma. She was walking down the Main Street sidewalk toward me.

I ran to her.

"You're okay?" she asked as she wrapped her arms around me.

"Yeah," I said. "I'm okay." I leaned back and looked her in the eyes. "Thank you. For everything."

"I'm just glad you're all—" She stopped when she saw my hand. "Your hand!"

I looked down. My hand was still bleeding from the knuckles. There was a lot of blood.

"I'm okay. Really."

"So, Betty's nephew, do you care to tell me what in holy heaven is going on here?" I turned to see Sheriff Daniels standing behind me.

"It's kind of complicated, sir," I said.

"Why don't you two follow me," the sheriff said, turning toward Cannova's.

We followed Sheriff Daniels toward Cannova's front door. Trish was being wheeled out on a stretcher. She looked upset. I'm sure she would've rather walked. Mike's mom was on the next stretcher. And Mike was being wheeled out behind her.

"Gosh, Furious. What happened?" Emma asked.

I was about to reply when Daniels turned around and said, "Yeah, Finbar. Or is it Furious? I'm curious too."

"It's Furious, sir. Furious Jones."

"Well, maybe you can show me what happened in there, Mr. Jones." The sheriff motioned inside.

"Okay," I said. But I didn't need to go inside. The entire sick scene was etched into my brain. The holes in Douglas's jacket. The look on Como's face and the giant gash in his neck. All of it. Every detail perfectly preserved in my messed-up mind.

We stepped into the restaurant and I started to tell the sheriff about my dad and his book. I told him about the assassin after Trish and her mom. I told him the assassin was dead on Cannova's kitchen floor. And I was just about to mention Attorney General Como's involvement when two EMTs rolled Douglas out on a stretcher. He was conscious but looked real bad. The stretcher left a trail of blood as it rolled across the restaurant floor.

"Who shot the CIA guy?" Daniels asked as we walked into the kitchen.

Anton and Como were lying on the floor in the middle of a growing pool of blood. Emma gasped.

"He did." I pointed to Como. "He shot Director Douglas."

Daniels crouched down next to Como. "Don't I know this guy?"

"You've probably seen him on TV. He's running for president," I said. "That's—"

"Attorney General Como," Daniels finished my sentence.

"Como?" Emma repeated. "Furious, how was the attorney general involved in all of this?"

"And who stuck that knife in his throat?" Daniels pointed to the butcher knife a few feet away.

"Trish did."

"Yeah," Daniels said. "That I can believe."

He looked back at me. "Let's take a ride over to Dubuque

and get your hand fixed up. You can tell me all about—" He stopped talking as he looked around the room. "All about whatever the hell this is."

The sheriff wrapped my hand in a bar towel, and we walked out onto Main Street.

"Hang on, I've got to grab something." Emma and Daniels watched as I walked over to Douglas's sedan and grabbed the photo album from the backseat.

I patted the cover of the album and said, "It's proof."

"Whatever." Daniels climbed into the truck.

Emma and I climbed into the backseat. I could see the flashing lights of an ambulance a few miles ahead of us. I hoped Trish's mom would be okay. Trish had been through enough.

"So, start from the beginning one more time," the sheriff said as he drove.

"Okay," I said. "The Chicago organized crime division has been cutting deals with members of the Salvatore crime syndicate for the last year. They offered a new life to anyone who would rat out fellow mob members. Dozens of bad guys and their families took them up on the offer, and the state ended up sending most of them to Galena."

"What?" Daniels asked. "Why wouldn't I have been told?"

"It sounds like no one was told. Maybe the state was worried about leaks, but somehow the FBI got wind of it. And apparently the Salvatore syndicate had a mole in the FBI who tipped off the Salvatores. So they sent their top assassin to Galena to kill the witnesses."

"Top assassin?" Daniels asked. "How do you know all of this?"

"Hang on, we'll get to that," I said.

"This is unbelievable, Furious," Emma said.

"Well, the FBI was unsure of whom they could trust, so they called in an agent from the CIA to help."

"I think I met the woman they sent," Daniels said.

"No, you met my mom. The guy they sent is now dead in one of those ambulances in front of us. The CIA sent a guy named Amado Anton, and his family, here to blend in and take the Salvatore assassins out. He had a unique talent for killing. He was perfect for this job. But, it turns out, Anton was working for the Salvatores."

"What kind of unique talent?" Emma asked.

"He made all the deaths look like accidents. Creative, bizarre accidents."

"Oh, dear god." The sheriff suddenly realized what had been going on in his town.

"The CIA sent my mom here after Anton was unable to stop the Salvatores."

"Right," Daniels agreed, "but Anton killed your mom."

"Yes."

"I met that CIA guy that you beat up after your mom was

killed," the sheriff said. "He seemed like a good enough guy."

"You beat up a CIA agent?" Emma asked.

"Kind of," I said. "His name is Director Douglas and he is, or was, the head of organized crime for the CIA."

"And you beat him up?" Emma asked again.

"Yes," I said. "Until tonight, I didn't know who to trust."

"So, tell me again," Daniels said. "How do you know all of this?"

"My dad," I said. "My dad is Robert Jones the author. My mom reached out to him for help before she died. He came to Galena to figure out who killed her. He was looking for justice. Or revenge. He put the truth about my mom's murder in his new book." I didn't mention the fact that all his previous books had also been about my mom's experiences. There was no need to tarnish his reputation now.

"I knew your dad," Daniels said. "I met him several times. He said he was here researching a book."

"He was," I said.

CHAPTER SIXTY-TWO

I *spent more than two hours having my hand stitched* up. I needed thirty-two stitches in all. Then a nurse escorted me to a waiting room on the second floor. Sheriff Daniels and Emma were sitting in overstuffed chairs by a window. Emma saw me and stood up.

"How bad was it?"

"Not bad," I lied.

"Twenty stitches?" Daniels guessed.

"Thirty-two," I said.

"Yeah, that was a nasty cut," Daniels said.

"Thirty-two stitches! My god, Furious!" Emma said.

"I'm fine. Any word on the others?"

"Yeah, the doctors were just out here a little bit ago,"

Emma said. "Trish is doing fine. Just a bunch of stitches too. But Mike has some damage to his foot. They're operating now."

"Trish had fewer stitches than you, Furious," Daniels said. "You should try getting shot next time."

"No, thanks. How about Trish's mom?"

Emma sighed. "No word yet. They said it looks like she's in a drug-induced coma, but there are no signs of drugs in her system."

"I guess that's why Anton was one of the best," I said. "Any word on Douglas?"

Emma perked up. "Yes. It sounds like he's doing fine. I mean, fine for having been shot several times. Apparently he was wearing a bulletproof vest."

"Yeah," Daniels interjected. "Believe me, being shot up close like that is still no picnic. He'll probably have some broken ribs, and depending on the ammo, the bullet may have still gone through the vest."

"But he'll be okay?" I asked.

"Yeah, he'll be okay," Emma repeated. "They're actually moving him into a room now. They said he could have visitors soon."

I sat down and we made small talk while I flipped through several magazines. A nurse came in twenty minutes later and said it was okay to go see Douglas. Sheriff Daniels stood up.

"I'd like to see him too," I said.

"Sure. I don't have any problem with that." He looked at Emma. "You can come on in too, darling."

The nurse led us down the hall to Douglas's room. They had removed the bandages from his face and replaced them with smaller ones. Most of his face was black and blue. It must have taken a lot of restraint for him not to shoot me in that front yard.

"Hey there," Daniels said as we walked in. "Thank god for Kevlar, eh, Douglas?"

"Zylon," Douglas said. "The vests are made of Zylon these days, Daniels. If it was Kevlar, I'd be dead."

"So I should throw out my old Kevlar vest?"

Douglas just shrugged.

"I called your superior," Daniels said. "What's his name, Hannahan?"

"Callahan," Douglas replied.

"Yeah, Callahan. He's sending someone out first thing in the morning."

"Did you tell him I was all right?"

"I said I thought you'd be all right."

"What about Como?" Douglas asked.

"Dead."

Douglas turned toward me. "How did you stop Como? Did you break his nose too?"

"No. I'm sorry about that." I motioned to his nose. "I wasn't sure what was going on. Didn't know who to trust."

"That makes two of us, kid."

"The girl, Trish—she knifed the attorney general," Daniels said.

Douglas murmured something.

"Are you up for giving a statement now?" Daniels asked.

"Can we do it tomorrow? Been kind of a long day."

"No sweat." Daniels stood up and looked at Emma and me. "Well, I guess I'll give you two a ride back to Galena."

"I'd like a minute with the kid," Douglas said, motioning to me.

"Okay. I'll be in the waiting room." Daniels walked out, but Emma and I didn't move.

"Who's your friend?" Douglas asked.

"A journalism friend of mine from Chicago. She came to help me," I said. "To tell the story of my dad's book and everything."

"Is that okay?" Emma asked.

"You're kind of young to be a reporter," Douglas said, wincing in pain.

"I'm a student journalist," Emma said, "but I'm good."

"Just do me a favor and leave Furious out of the story," Douglas said.

"Why?" I asked.

"'Cause the world thinks you're dead," Douglas said, "and that's probably for the best."

"But what about me? How does a dead guy live?"

Douglas didn't answer. He just stared at me.

"Witness protection?" I asked. "In my experience, witness protection doesn't offer so much protection."

Douglas looked at Emma and said, "Will you please excuse us? I need to talk to Furious alone."

Emma looked at me, and I nodded that it was okay.

Emma left the room and Douglas said, "I was very fond of your mother, Furious. She was a wonderful woman and a wonderful agent."

I said nothing.

Douglas continued, "And you remind me a lot of her. A lot. Except you were able to do something that neither your mom nor your dad could do."

"What's that?" I asked.

"You stopped Anton."

"Actually, Como stopped Anton," I said.

"But you put the pieces together and came to Galena to get justice," Douglas said. "Against all odds."

"I had nothing left to lose. My entire family is gone."

Douglas quietly nodded his head.

"I know I'm a stranger to you, Furious. But I've known you your entire life. I cared about your mom, and I care about you."

I wasn't sure what to say to that. Here was a complete stranger who was saying he cared. "Thank you," I said.

"Join us, Furious."

"What are you talking about?" I asked. "I'm only twelve."

"That doesn't matter. Join us and I'll train you. I'll take care of you. Believe it or not, we sometimes recruit agents as young as you. They all do it. The Russians. The Brits. There are special projects that require certain attributes and skills."

"Are you serious?" I couldn't believe what I was hearing. Me, a spy for the CIA? "I have no skills."

"You have more skills than you realize, and I can teach you the rest. I'm forming a new team, and you would be perfect on it."

"Who else is on this team?" I asked, but Douglas just stared at me. "Ah, top secret, right?"

Douglas gave a little nod and winced in pain again.

"Will you be going after the Salvatores? The people that destroyed my family?"

"Yes," Douglas said. "And I hope to get them. But we could use your help."

A nurse walked in and asked Douglas how he felt.

"Like I went through a meat grinder," he said.

"Don't say 'meat grinder.'" I laughed.

"Look, kid, I'm going to get a little rest. Let's continue this conversation in a little bit."

CHAPTER SIXTY-THREE

Emma *got a ride from Sheriff Daniels and headed* back to Chicago to write the story, and I fell asleep in the waiting room and slept until almost eight o'clock. There were several families in the room when I woke up.

I walked out into the hall and asked a nurse if I could see Mike and Trish.

"I think that would be okay. But let me check." She disappeared into a room down the hall and reappeared several minutes later. "Sure, sweetie. Go on in."

I pushed the door open. Trish's mom was in the bed. The room was dark. I waved to Trish who was sitting in a chair next to her mom. Mike was on a small couch with his foot elevated in a cast.

"Hey, man," he whispered. "How are you feeling?"

"Oh, I'm fine. How about you?" I motioned to his foot.

"I'm fine, considering I was shot and all."

"And your mom?"

"They still don't know," Trish said, "but she's stable now." I nodded.

"Look at your hair," Trish said. "Have you been here all night?"

I ran my good hand through my snarled mess. I needed a haircut. "Yeah. I've been waiting to see how you guys are doing."

"I think she's going to be okay." Trish quickly added, "She's tough."

"Like someone else I know," I said.

No one spoke for several minutes. I sat and listened to the beeps and hums of hospital equipment.

I finally said, "I'm heading out."

"Okay. Are you going to stop back later?" Mike asked.

"No. I mean—I'm leaving."

Mike said, "Okay, dude. I'd get up and all, but you know." He pointed to his foot.

"Yeah, I know—you're lazy." I smiled, walked over, and shook his hand.

"You'll be in touch, right?" Mike asked.

"You bet," I said. And who knew? Maybe I would be.

Trish stood up and I walked to her.

"Thank you," I said. "You saved my life."

"I think it's the other way around, Amos."

I gave her a long hug and walked out without looking back.

CHAPTER SIXTY-FOUR

I **walked outside and sat on a hospital bench. I had** nothing. No family. No home. Nothing but an offer from Douglas. And it was tempting. The Salvatores had destroyed my life and countless others. And the guy who'd killed my grandpa right before my eyes was still out there. If I went with Douglas, maybe I'd have a chance to avenge his death. But maybe it was all BS. A twelve-year-old in the CIA? It seemed crazy. And where would I live? In some sort of government foster care? No, thanks.

I pulled out my wallet. I had two bucks. If I *was* going to leave, I'd have to leave now. Before more CIA showed up. But I'd need money to get away. I searched my phone for a bank. My bank had a Dubuque branch. And it was only a few blocks from the hospital. I guessed that everything was only a few blocks in Dubuque.

I started walking. Maybe they could give me a replacement card. I had, like, $400 in my account. Maybe it would be enough to get out of the Midwest.

I found the branch on the corner of Main and Third. The manager assured me that cards went missing all the time and he would have me up and running in no time. I showed him my ID and he excused himself and returned a minute later with a new card.

"Okay, just go ahead and swipe the card through the machine and enter your PIN."

I slid the new card through the machine on his desk and entered my code.

"Perfect, Mr. Jones." He turned the monitor toward him and began typing. "And which accounts would you like associated with the card?"

"I only have one account," I said. "It's got, like, four hundred bucks in it."

"Yes, your primary checking." He clicked some more keys. "It looks like there are several new accounts listing you as a joint tenant."

"Joint tenant?" I repeated.

"Yes, accounts you share with Robert Jones?"

"My dad? Go ahead and associate all the accounts," I

said. My dad must have added me to his accounts before he died. Maybe he knew the Salvatore family would never let him and *Double Crossed* get away with exposing their operation.

"Will do," the banker said, clicking a few more keys. "There you go, Mr. Jones. It is ready to use any time. Is there anything else I can assist you with today?"

"Is there any way you could raise my daily withdrawal limit to, say, three thousand dollars?" I figured there had to be at least three thousand among all the accounts.

"Sure, no problem. Anything else?"

I stood up. "Yes, does Dubuque have an airport?"

"Oh, yes. You can get most anywhere in the country from Dubuque via Chicago O'Hare."

"How far away is it?" I asked.

"Oh, just drive right down Highway 61. You can't miss it. It's probably a twenty-minute drive."

Great, I thought. *That's, like, a two-hour walk.*

"Thanks," I said.

I stopped at the bank's lobby ATM on my way out. I stuck my card in, entered my code, and punched the balance button. I was presented with three account numbers. I touched the first account and saw a balance of $386. My primary checking. I selected the next account, and the machine said I had more than seventy thousand dollars in that account. I selected the final account. Wow! This must have been from my dad's estate. Or maybe it was his entire estate. It said I had a lifetime of money.

I took out three thousand dollars and walked back to the manager's desk.

"Excuse me, does Dubuque have a taxi service?"

CHAPTER SIXTY-FIVE

*T*he cab dropped me off at the Dubuque Regional Airport. I tipped the cabbie ten bucks and walked inside. There was a little café directly in front of me. I was starving. I ordered a Coke and scanned the menu for something to eat.

The girl behind the counter brought me my Coke and asked, "Can I get you anything else?"

"Ah, you don't have any scones, do you?"

"Absolutely. What kind?"

"What do you have?"

"Blueberry, lemon, and cinnamon."

"Perfect. I'll take one of each."

I sat down at a table to eat all three scones when my phone buzzed once. It was Emma.

"Hey, how is my favorite journalist?"

"Pretty awesome, actually." Emma sounded excited.

"Yeah? Did you write the story of the year?" I asked.

"More like the story of the decade," she said. "They're running my story in the *Chicago Tribune* today, Furious. Can you believe that? On the front page, no less!"

"Of course they are," I said, smiling. "You're good."

"Mrs. Dalton, the woman who runs the program here at Northwestern, she said it was as fine a piece of investigative journalism as she has ever seen from a student."

"That's awesome, Em. You deserve it."

"It's all thanks to you. How are you doing? How is Trish's mom?"

"She's not out of the woods yet, but they think she's going to be okay," I said.

"And you?" Emma asked. "How are you doing?"

"I'm all right." *Other than I lost everything in my life*, I thought.

"What happens to you now?"

"I'm thinking I might disappear for a while. Think things through a bit," I said.

"Will you let me know where you disappear to?"

"As long as you don't report it," I said.

"Anonymity is part of the craft," Emma said. "Besides, as far as my readers are concerned, Furious Jones is dead." She paused and then added, "I can't believe I have readers!"

"I can. I'll call you as soon as I settle someplace," I said.

"Okay. Take care of yourself."

"You too."

And then, almost as if on cue, my cheap, crappy phone died. I stood up and threw the Coke can and the cheap phone in the trash.

I passed a newspaper stand on my way to the ticketing counter. Large stacks of my dad's new book, *Double Crossed*, were piled out front. I grabbed a copy and handed it to the clerk.

"I hear Carson Kidd actually dies in this book," the clerk said, pointing to the cover.

"Yeah, I heard something like that too," I said.

I paid for the book and walked toward the ticketing counter. I stared at the photo of my dad on the back of the book while waiting in line. He looked like the big man. Like a world famous adventurer, fearless explorer, tough-guy author. And in the end, he was. He did the right thing. He stood up to the bad guys and tried to fix the wrongs.

"Sir? Sir?" The man behind the counter was motioning to me.

"How can I help you?"

"Yes. One ticket, please."

"To where, sir?"

I looked back down at my dad. I had spent most of my life wanting to make him proud. Wanting him to notice me.

"To where, sir?" the man behind the counter asked again.

"Ahhh . . ."

CHAPTER SIXTY-SIX

I *pushed the door open and walked into Douglas's* room.

"I've got one condition," I said.

Douglas looked shocked to see me. "And what's that?"

"I'll do it if you promise that we'll nail each and every one of those Salvatores."

Douglas smiled. "With you onboard, Furious, I believe we will."

"Then I'm in."